The Sign of Four

by Sir Arthur Conan Doyle

A Study Guide by Ray Moore M.A.

Picture: Sherlock Holmes (1904) by Sidney Paget (1860-1908). This picture is in the public domain and therefore free of copyright restrictions

Copyright

Contents

Preface   3

The Detective Story: Birth of a Genre 5

Elements of the Classic Detective Mystery: 9

The Sherlock Holmes Canon 12

Dramatis Personae - List of Characters   17

Sherlock Holmes: 17

Dr. John H. Watson: 18

Other Characters: 20

Historical Background: 23

The East India Company - A Brief Timeline: 23

The Indian Mutiny of 1857 to 1858 - A Brief Timeline: 23

The Andaman Island Prison - A Brief Timeline: 24

The Sign of Four by Sir Arthur Conan Doyle   25

Chapter I: The Science of Deduction 25

Chapter II: The Statement of the Case 28

Chapter III: In Quest of a Solution...30

Chapter IV: The Story of the Bald-Headed Man 32

Chapter V: The Tragedy of Pondicherry Lodge 35

Chapter VI: Sherlock Holmes Gives a Demonstration 37

Chapter VII: The Episode of the Barrel 40

Chapter VIII: The Baker Street Irregulars 42

Chapter IX: A Break in the Chain...44

Chapter X: The End of the Islander 46

Chapter XI: The Great Agra Treasure...48

Chapter XII: The Strange Story of Jonathan Small 50

Studying the Novel   55

   Chronology of the Case..55

   Picking Faults...56

   Structure of a Sherlock Holmes Mystery 63

   The Scientific Detective 65

   The Character of Sherlock Holmes 70

   The Character of Dr. Watson 73

   British Colonialism 74

Appendix One: Brief Summaries of the Other Sherlock Holmes Novels   76

Appendix Two: Character Traits (Student Activities)   76

   Character of Sherlock Holmes 77

   Sherlock Holmes as Detective 78

   Character of Dr. Watson 79

Appendix Three: The Scientific Detective (Student Activities)   80

   1. Two Examples of the Methods of Sherlock Holmes in Chapter One 80

   2. The History of the Crime 82

   3. Examining the Scene of the Crime...87

   Finding the Fugitives and the Treasure 90

   Possible explanations for the Disappearance of the Aurora............................91

   How to Catch Jonathan Small 91

Guide to Further Reading   92

To the Reader   94

Preface

The Sign of Four (sometimes titled *The Sign of The Four*) was Sir Arthur Conan Doyle's second Sherlock Holmes novel (the first being *A Study in Scarlet*), written before Doyle thought of writing short stories for the magazine market featuring Holmes and Watson. Doyle from the start had no illusion that he was writing great (or even serious) literature. The Holmes stories began as, and continued to be, 'potboilers' - popular fiction which gave Doyle the financial security that enabled him to concentrate on the historical fiction on which he felt that his literary reputation would depend. Indeed, it is well known that later in his career Doyle would make several attempts to terminate the Holmes stories, all of which failed due to the popularity of Holmes.

Although the novel should be read first and foremost as the sensational detective and adventure story it was intended to be, there is a lot more to examine. The novel is crucial in the development of the detective mystery genre, and it tells us a great deal about late Victorian attitudes to empire, race and social class. In addition, when viewed as a work of art, the novel is far from perfect having multiple inconsistencies and improbabilities. At times, therefore, this Guide takes a highly critical look at aspects of the novel.

The aim of this Study Guide is to encourage the reader to think about this text and to reach his/her own conclusions. If you are looking for a Guide that simply tells you what to think, this is probably not the book for you. However, in order effectively to reflect on this text, the contemporary reader needs information on the early development of the detective genre, and historical background concerning the sections of the story set in India. These are provided, together with an annotated list of all of the characters in the novel. In addition, for each chapter there is a commentary, which draws attention to matters of interest and importance. Finally, graphic organizers are provided to assist the reader in making notes.

The most important single element of the book is the guiding questions. These are *not* designed to test the reader, but to help him/her to locate and to understand characters, plot, settings, and themes in the text. They do not normally have simple answers, nor is there always one answer. Consider a range of possible interpretations - preferably by discussing the questions with others. Disagreement is to be encouraged! Effective reading is *active reading*, and the active reader constantly asks questions of the text. The basic question that a reader should ask of any text is:

HOW

DO THE WORDS ON THE PAGE

CREATE THE MEANING

I GET WHEN I READ THE PAGE?

Much of the material in this Guide is adapted from my book *The Sign of Four by Sir Arthur Conan Doyle: Text and Critical Introduction* (published February 2015) which presents the full text together with detailed notes and vocabulary.

Dedication:

At a time when those who work in public education are so frequently criticized by commentators and politicians who have themselves never taught and would probably not last fifteen minutes in front of a class of thirty youngsters, I want to dedicate this book to all of those who work in the public school system.

In a career of 38 years as a classroom teacher in public schools both in the U.K. and the U.S.A., I have seen ample evidence of the dedication and professionalism of administrators, teachers, and ancillary staff who strive to give children the best possible start in life.

Acknowledgements:

I am indebted to the work of numerous editors, biographers, and critics as I have acknowledged in the Bibliography. Once again, I stand on the shoulders of giants. Where I am conscious of having taken an idea or a phrase from a particular author, I have cited the source in the text. Any failure to do so is an omission which I will correct immediately if it is drawn to my attention.

The text of *The Sign of Four* is in the public domain and is not, therefore, subject to copyright. Where I have selectively quoted from the writings of others in the course of my own argument, I have done so in the sincere belief that this constitutes fair use.

Thanks, as always, are due to my wife, Barbara, for putting the text into the correct formats for publication, and to John for reading the manuscript and offering valuable suggestions. Any errors which remain are my own.

Illustrations

All illustrations by Sidney Paget are, to the best of my knowledge, in the public domain.

The Detective Story: Birth of a Genre

The detective story is so popular today that, without thinking about it, we tend to assume that the genre has always been around. Surprisingly, detective mysteries are (with one controversial exception) a relatively modern literary innovation dating back only to the middle of the nineteenth century.

In some ways, the first detective mystery in world literature is the Classical Greek tragedy *Oedipus Rex* by Sophocles, which was first performed circa 429 B.C.. Oedipus, King of Thebes, is informed by the Oracle at Delphi that the plague which is ravaging his city will only end when the murderer of the previous king, Laius, is discovered and brought to justice. Oedipus (the first detective in the first 'Whodunit?') conducts a thorough enquiry by questioning all of the witnesses still living and assembling the evidence. This logical approach points unerringly to Oedipus himself as the murderer and the process uncovers even more terrible truths about Oedipus' past. Racked by guilt, the King blinds himself and leaves the city in self-imposed exile. Of course, Sophocles was not consciously writing a detective mystery; he was re-telling an ancient myth the theme of which was the punishment of Oedipus' hubris in trying to defy the will of the Gods. Moreover, since every member of the original audiences would already have known the myth, the drama has none of the tension of the modern mystery which derives from the parallel efforts of the detective and the reader to identify the perpetrator. In fact, the main effect of the play is dramatic irony since, unlike the audience, Oedipus does not know the truth which he is about to uncover. Nevertheless, the play has so many of the elements of modern crime fiction that it is remarkable that no other detective mystery would be written for well over two thousand years.

Elizabethan and Jacobean drama is replete with crimes, particularly murder, and the first true novels, written by Daniel Defoe (*The Life of Jonathan Wild* [1725], *Moll Flanders* [1722], etc.), are full of crime and corruption, but are entirely without mystery since the identity of the perpetrator is never in doubt. The *Newgate Calendar*, originally a monthly bulletin of executions, produced by the keeper of Newgate prison in London, was a hugely popular publication between 1750 and 1850 because of its sensational descriptions of the most heinous crimes and the punishments of the (supposedly) guilty. What is missing, at least until the later versions of the Calendar, is any "idea of rational inquiry leading to the containment of crime" (Knight 15). Thus, neither in life nor in fiction is there a single example, official or unofficial, of a detective figure until the middle of the nineteenth century. Malefactors were either caught in the act, or condemned by the unanimous opinion of their neighbors, or they confessed - and no doubt a lot of innocent people were convicted and imprisoned or hanged. Before the middle of the nineteenth century, there was also a tendency to romanticize criminals (the mythical ride from London to York of highwayman

Dick Turpin is but one example) as rebels against an oppressive government fated, if captured, to endure cruel and unusual punishments.

In fiction, the detective mystery as a genre had its origins in the mid-nineteenth century as an off-shoot of the Romantic Gothic novel, a genre that combined horror and romance: "Prominent features of Gothic fiction include terror (both psychological and physical), mystery, the supernatural, ghosts, haunted houses and Gothic architecture, castles, darkness, death, decay, doubles, madness, secrets and hereditary curses" (Wikipedia). The first Gothic novel is usually taken to be Horace Walpole's *The Castle of Otranto* (1764); Ann Radcliffe's *The Mysteries of Udolpho* (1794) was the most popular example; and Jane Austen satirized the genre in *Northanger Abbey* (1803). King points to Landrum's count of seventy novels published between 1794 and 1854 which had the word "mystery" in their titles, though the term was not, as yet, attached to a single, unsolved crime (19).

Although claims have been made for earlier authors, the American writer Edgar Allan Poe (1809-1849), whose short stories were usually of the horror genre involving death, decay, and madness, is generally credited with writing the first true detective story in 1841. This was the "The Murders in the Rue Morgue" which features a terrible double murder in Paris: a mother and daughter are found brutally murdered in a room where all of the windows are locked from the inside and access to the windows from the outside is clearly impossible given the height of the building and the total absence of handholds. The amateur detective Chevalier C. Auguste Dupin, "the first fictional investigator to rely primarily on deduction from observable facts" (James 33), solves a mystery which completely defeats the French police. Knight explains Poe's contribution to the detective mystery thus:

> [H]is detective stories ... were to bring together for the first time the Gothic melodrama that had been a major element in early crime fiction with the concept of a clever explanatory figure who had not appeared before ... Poe saw the possibilities that others were only half grasping, and ... constructed a form strong enough to predict the possibilities of the genre that was not yet in being. (25-6)

Dupin himself terms his method "ratiocination." His debut was followed by the stories "The Mystery of Marie Rogêt" (1842-3) and "The Purloined Letter" (1845).

In France, the period 1840-1860 saw a rapid expansion of tales involving detective figures by serious authors such as Honoré de Balzac, Alexandre Dumas, and Émile Gaboriau (who is usually credited as "the creator of the detective novel" [Priestman in Hodgson ed. 313]), but in England the genre developed much more slowly. Notable examples include Delf's *The Detective's Notebook* (1860) and Forrester's *The Female Detective* (1864), but none of these came close to the classic detective mystery. Thus, while Charles Dickens' novels feature both criminals and detectives, both are incidental to the main plots. *Bleak House* (1852-3) includes the character Inspector Bucket, a detective who undertakes several investigations including that of Mr. Tulkinghorn's murder, which he brings to a successful conclusion, and the pursuit of the fleeing Lady Deadlock, who he is not able to find in time to save her life. Dickens' final novel *The Mystery of Edwin Drood* (1870) appears to have a potential detective figure, but it remained unfinished at his death, and so the author's intentions remain unclear.

The credit for a definite movement in English fiction in the direction of the modern detective mystery is usually given to Wilkie Collins. In both *The Woman in White* (1859) and *The Moonstone* (1868) crimes are solved by solid detective work (together with a fair measure of luck and coincidence). *The Moonstone* was termed by T. S. Eliot "the first and greatest of English detective novels," and Dorothy Sayers called it "probably the very finest detective story ever written" (Knight 44). The story involves the disappearance of the fabled diamond called The Moonstone from the room of Rachel Verinder. The local police are baffled and gladly hand over the case to the famous Sergeant Cuff of London who makes great strides toward solving the mystery. However, Cuff is removed from the case at a crucial point and only reappears towards the end of the novel when others have made more progress in explaining the disappearance of the jewel. Both *The Woman in White* and *The Moonstone* employ multiple narrators so there is no single controlling consciousness. The crimes are solved not by one person but by a number of characters whose separate efforts come together in an amazing revelation of the truth and in the just punishment for the offenders.

Even though Collins did not give to the genre the central detective figure which is its single most essential element, P. D. James notes that he "is meticulously accurate in his treatment of medical and forensic details. There is an emphasis on the importance of physical clues - a bloodstained nightdress, a smeared door, a metal chain - and all the clues are made available to the reader ..." (21). What Collins had done, Henry James pointed out, was to bring the sensationalism of the Gothic novel to the familiar landscape of England:

> To Mr. Collins belongs the credit of having introduced into fiction those most mysterious of mysteries, the mysteries which are at our own doors. This innovation ... was fatal to the authority of Mrs. Radcliffe [1764-1823, writer of many Gothic novels most famously *The Mysteries of Udolpho*] and her everlasting castle in the Apennines. What are the Apennines to us or we to the Apennines? Instead of the terrors of "Udolpho," we were treated to the terrors of the cheerful country-house and the best London lodgings. And there is no doubt that these were infinitely more terrible. (*The Nation*)

However, neither Inspector Bucket nor Sergeant Cuff, both being middle class members of the official police force, fits the model of the gentleman (or less often the gentlewoman) amateur detective.

In the final decade of the nineteenth century, Sir Arthur Conan Doyle's creation, Sherlock Holmes, achieved great popularity with the British reading public. Doyle wrote that his main achievement was to replace crime novels in which the solution was arrived at by luck or chance through the creation of "a scientific detective who solved cases on his own merits and not through the folly of the criminal" (Hodgson ed. 3). Neilson disagrees, indicating that Doyle's essential contribution to the detective genre was not in the mechanics of the plot or in the nature of criminal detection, but in "his 'humanizing' of the detective. Edgar Allan Poe's C. Auguste Dupin is little more than a disembodied intellect. Collins's Sergeant Cuff is more personable but considerably less skillful. Émile Gaboriau's two early examples, Monsieur Lecoq and Père Tabaret, are ingenious detectives and amiable fellows, but they have almost no distinguishing personal traits" (*Masterplots*). In contrast, Holmes is both a thinker and a man of action, a player of the violin and a talented boxer. Moreover, he is a detective who evidently derives great pleasure from solving puzzles. Not only are both men correct, but Holmes' methods and his personality are seamlessly intertwined.

That Doyle, a voracious reader from his childhood, was well aware of the precursors we have examined is evident in *The Sign of Four* which draws so directly on both Poe and Collins that the charge of plagiarism might be made. Doyle and Crowder suggest that the murder of Bartholomew Sholto in his inaccessible, upper storey room has obvious parallels with, and was indeed inspired by, Poe's "The Murders in the Rue Morgue" (30). They also show the extent of Doyle's debt to Collins by using parallel quotation to prove that he borrowed many of Cuff's physical features in his descriptions of Sherlock Holmes (25). Even more specifically, the novel clearly borrows from *The Moonstone* its central plot device of a fabulous treasure stolen from India and pursued from there by those determined to return it to its 'rightful' owners.

The huge success of the Holmes novels and short stories caused many writers to imitate Doyle's narrative methods. The first half of the twentieth century was the great age of the amateur detective - the individual with supreme insight who could see behind the deceptions of the most cunning criminal. You have to remember that this was a time when the scientific investigation of crime was in its infancy. Solving a crime rested on establishing: Means, Motive and Opportunity (or, to put it another way: How? Why? and When?). In the age before sophisticated forensics, this could be discovered by careful observation, judicious questioning, and the ability to make logical connections. It was also during this period that murder became *the* crime in detective fiction. The number of murders which Holmes investigates is surprisingly small; indeed, some of his most intriguing cases involve no crime at all.

The most famous writer of what came to be called the Golden Age of Detective Fiction, which spanned the time period between World War I and World War II, was Agatha Christie (1891-1976) whose two most popular creations were the Belgian detective Hercule Poirot and the spinster Miss Marple. A contemporary of Christie's, the writer Raymond Chandler (1888-1959), added the American Private Detective to the genre through his hero Philip Marlowe. American detective stories were, from the start, more violent, more 'hard-boiled,' than their English equivalents.

Since the Second World War, much more variety has been introduced into detective fiction, though one trend which is common to most stories of the genre is an increased concern with getting the details of criminal investigation right even as police procedures have become more complex and their methods more scientific. This has resulted in stories that are generally realistic and unromantic. Police Procedurals have a professional policeman or woman as the central figure and follow closely established methods of investigation. The 87th Precinct novels of Ed McBain, featuring New York detective Steve Carella, are a good example.

Elements of the Classic Detective Mystery:

> What we can expect is a central mysterious crime, usually murder; a closed circle of suspects, each with motive, means and opportunity for the crime; a detective, either amateur or professional, who comes in like an avenging deity to solve it; and, by the end of the book, a solution which the reader should be able to arrive at by logical deduction from clues inserted in the novel with deceptive cunning but essential fairness [...] It is an inviolable rule that the detective should never know more than the reader." (James 9 & 59)

The classic detective mystery contains the following elements:

1. Crime: A crime (normally a murder) is committed by one (or more) of a small number of people, all of whom have possible motives.

2. Setting: The setting is usually an isolated location which effectively restricts the range of possible suspects and makes it equally impossible for the suspects to leave or for outside help to arrive. (The titles of two of Agatha Christie's novels will illustrate this type of setting: *Murder on the Orient Express* and *Death on the Nile*. In each of these stories, the number of suspects is limited to the people travelling on either the train or the boat respectively. Another of her stories is set in a house on a small island off the coast of England.)

3. Characters: There are a fixed and relatively small number of characters each of whom appears to have a motive for the crime as well as the means and opportunity to commit it.

4. Plot structure: The author deliberately plants 'red-herrings' (false clues) in order to confuse the reader, to lead him/her to suspect the wrong people, and to reduce the chances of the reader noting the one or two significant clues which actually solve the mystery. Sometimes the writer 'cheats' by allowing the detective access to information which the reader does not have.

5. The detective: Originally a man, though increasingly a woman, of formidable intellect who is able to piece together the evidence of means, motive and opportunity in order to reveal the guilty party. (Although the genre originated with the talented amateur sleuth [Holmes, Father Brown, Lord Peter Whimsy, Miss Marple, etc.] who outsmarts the official police, as crime detection has become more technical and scientific the sleuth has more often been a professional detective [Inspector Morse, Detective Steve Carella, Detective Chief-Inspector Adam Dalgliesh, etc.]. In such cases, the detective is usually something of an individualist whose approach to solving crimes is very different from that of his colleagues.)

6. The detective's friend: Many detectives, of course, work alone, but a surprising number work together with a close friend. This is normally a man of a practical nature but no skill in detection who performs three functions: he is able to attend to practical matters for which the detective has neither the time nor the inclination; his inability to make logical deductions shows, by contrast, the skills of the detective; and his limited understanding provides the author with an excuse for getting the detective to explain his reasoning. Additionally, the friend (following the tradition inaugurated by Dr. Watson) is often the narrator of the stories.

7. The innocent accused: All of the evidence points to this person, although it is clear to the reader, and to the detective, that he/she is innocent.

8. The Police: Whether the detective figure is an amateur, a private investigator or a policeman, a contrast is drawn between his/her methods and those of the official police. The latter always do things 'by the Book,' and as a result miss everything which is not blindingly obvious. Again, their inability shows up the skills of the detective by contrast.

9. Delayed denouement: Rosemary Jann points to this paradox of detective stories:

> they move toward solution but exist only so long as closure can be postponed. Our reading pleasure is intimately tied to the suspense that this postponement creates ... Once the mystery has been devised,

the author's main problem is one of concealment: how to limit the revelation of the solution long enough to maintain the reader's interest. (22-3)

A number of narrative strategies are used to ensure that the solution is kept from the reader. The obtuse narrator (usually a friend of the detective), a person who records every detail without being conscious of what the clues actually are, is the most obvious of these. Others include the false trails followed by the official police, the innocent suspect, and (that most abused of all techniques) the 'red herrings' planted by author.

10. The climax: The detective gathers together all of the suspects for a final, dramatic explanation of the who, how and why of the crime which culminates in the naming of the guilty person, who then confesses.

11. The fate of the guilty person: In more modern stories, he/she is most likely to be handed over to the forces of law for trial and punishment, but in earlier stories the amateur detective sometimes allows a higher form of justice to take its course (e.g., the criminal commits suicide or, at the other extreme, is found to have been so justified in what he/she did that he/she is allowed to go free). This is common in the Sherlock Holmes stories.

Of course, writers of detective mysteries have never slavishly used the above points as a template, but one of the great attractions of the genre for readers is its predictability. Most Agatha Christie novels, for example, follow this general formula. Her detectives typically uncover a tangled web of motivation and causation which often goes back several years, sometimes decades. Paradoxically, the Sherlock Holmes stories, whether in the form of novels or short stories, seldom follow the very template that they were inventing (though *The Hound of the Baskervilles* comes closest to it).

Quintessentially, the detective story involves the reader in solving a puzzle. The reader is effectively in a race with the detective to sort out which of the suspects, all of whom appear to have had motive, actually also had the means and the opportunity to do the crime/murder. Of the characters in the story, the detective alone is able to see through the alibi of the guilty one(s). Therefore, the test of a good detective mystery is that the reader does not guess the identity of the perpetrator despite having been given *all* of the clues in the course of the narrative. When the real criminal is unmasked, the reader should initially be surprised but then realize that it had to be him/her all along!

The 'Whodunit?' plot-line, however, by no means exhausts the possibilities of the detective mystery. In some detective stories, it is perfectly clear from the start who the criminal is and what his or her motives are. What remains to be discovered is *how* the crime was committed. Many of the Holmes stories are of this type, the villain being identified immediately by his (or, much less often, her) physical descriptions and manner. Perhaps the most famous such story is

The Speckled Band. Helen Stoner's sister has been found dead just before she was to be married, and now the young woman fears for her own life. It is perfectly clear to the reader that the culprit is Helen's violent stepfather, Sir Grimesby Roylott, whose financial motives are not difficult to determine. The mystery lies in watching Holmes discover the manner in which the murder was performed, and specifically what the dying sister mean when she cried, "The band! The speckled band!"

Another variation is a story in which it is immediately clear to the reader who committed the crime and how that person did it, but it is by no means clear what possible *motive* they had for doing so. Finally (though I am sure that there must be still other variations), there is the plot where the reader is told precisely who did it, and how and why they did it. Since the crime appears to have been meticulously planned and executed (i.e., the near-perfect crime), the mystery and accompanying suspense lies in finding out *how* the detective will discover the truth and bring the criminal to justice. If you have ever seen re-runs of the *Colombo* series, you will know exactly how this variation works.

Any of the variations described above may involve what is often regarded as the holy grail of detective fiction, the 'locked room mystery' in which the crime (again most often murder) has been committed in a room which appears to have been totally secure so that no one could have entered it to commit the crime and (more importantly) no one could not possibly have got out of the room having done it. Needless to say, crime writers have discovered endless ways of solving this particular mystery. *The Sign of Four* certainly features a murder in a room which appears, at first, to be entirely inaccessible. (Doyle's solution borrows heavily from Poe's use of an Ourang-Outang as the murderer in "The Murders in the Rue Morgue.")

The Sherlock Holmes Canon

Novels:
>   *A Study in Scarlet (*1887 in Beeton's Christmas Annual),
>   *The Sign of [the] Four* (1890 in Lippincott's Monthly Magazine),
>   *The Hound of the Baskervilles* (1901-02 in The Strand Magazine),
>   *The Valley of Fear* (1914-15 in The Strand Magazine).

Collections of short stories:
>   *The Adventures of Sherlock Holmes* (twelve stories from The Strand Magazine 1891-2),
>   *The Memoirs of Sherlock Holmes* (twelve stories from The Strand Magazine 1894),
>   *The Return of Sherlock Holmes* (thirteen stories originally published 1903-04),
>   *His Last Bow* (seven stories originally published 1908-1917),

The Sign of Four by Sir Arthur Conan Doyle

The Case-Book of Sherlock Holmes (twelve stories from The Strand Magazine 1921-27).

The idea that Doyle began writing fiction because he had so few patients in the practice which he opened in July 1882 at 1, Bush Villas, Elm Grove, Portsmouth, is largely a myth. Even today, any new medical practice takes some time to establish a regular clientele, and at first patients were indeed few and far between. In his first year, Doyle earned only £154, but in his second the figure rose to £250, and in his third to £300, which was around the average income for a doctor in general practice at that time (Booth 95-6). Nor is it true that Doyle was not a particularly good doctor and took little interest in his profession. In fact, he submitted numerous articles to medical journals, proved himself to be, both in terms of his relationships with patients and his medical knowledge, somewhat ahead of his time, and began to specialize in diseases of the eye. However, in 1891, a serious attack of influenza, the failure of his eye specialist practice in Upper Wimpole Street, London, the increasing sums paid for his Holmes stories, and the critical success of his historical novel *The White Company* combined to persuade Doyle that literature would subsequently be his sole means of earning a living. (He would return to medicine during the Boer War as a volunteer.)

In his excellent biography of Doyle, Martin Booth draws on the author's own article in the *Westminster Gazette* (December 1900) to give the following account of the inception of the first Holmes novel, *A Study in Scarlet*:

> [T]he idea of writing about a detective came to him around 1886 when he had read some detective stories and thought they were nonsensical because the plots, often thin, unimaginative and imitative, either revolved around coincidence or relied for their denouement on the authors revealing vital clues that had previously been hidden from the readers ... [T]he detectives themselves were stereotypes who lacked depth and did not display their lines of deduction. He wanted to create, he said, "a scientific detective, who solved cases on his own merits and not through the folly of the criminal. (104)

In the novel's planning stages, the detective was first called Sherringford Holmes then Sherrington Hope, and the doctor Ormond Sacker. Scholars have made many suggestions as to the origin of the names Sherlock Holmes and Dr. John Watson, but as readers we may simply be glad of the change!

Although Doyle had no thought when writing *A Study in Scarlet* that it would be the first of a series of stories (and certainly not of a series which would span forty years), in all he would write four Holmes novels and fifty-six short stories, all of which appeared as serials or as part of a series in monthly magazines before being published as books. Having been rejected by a number of publishers, the copyright of *A Study in Scarlet* was purchased for £25 by

Beeton's Christmas Annual. Having sold the copyright, Doyle did not make a penny more on that novel.

Although the creation of Holmes ultimately made Conan Doyle a very rich man, he saw himself initially as a writer of serious historical fiction (*Micah Clarke* [1889], *The White Company* [1891], *Rodney Stone* [1896] etc.), later on in his career as an historian (*The War in South Africa - Its Causes and Conduct* [1902], *The British Campaign in France and Flanders* [6 vols. 1916-20], etc.), and still later as a writer on Spiritualism (*The New Revelation* [1918], *The Case for Spirit Photography* [1922], etc.). To Doyle, the Holmes stories were merely 'potboilers,' designed to cater to the public taste and, of course, to make money. Once Doyle had secured a steady income from royalties, at various points in his career Doyle would became impatient with the constant public clamor for more Holmes stories. Indeed, as Cox points out, the ending of *The Sign of Four* indicates that Doyle had, at that time, no thought of writing more Sherlock Holmes stories:

> Even though the story demonstrates that Conan Doyle had his formula fully under control, we can see that he had no plans to continue the saga. Watson's marriage will separate Holmes from his chronicler and the 'series' will end with the second and final story. (48)

As with *A Study in Scarlet* which preceded it, *The Sign of Four* was not met with universal approval in contemporary reviews. The Athenaeum review of December 6th, 1890, read:

> A detective story is usually lively reading, but we cannot pretend to think that 'The Sign of Four' is up to the level of the writer's best work. It is a curious medley, full or horrors; and surely those who play at hide and seek with the fatal treasure are a strange company. The wooden-legged convict and his fiendish misshapen little mate, the ghastly twins, the genial prizefighters, the detectives wise and foolish, and the gentle girl whose lover tells the tale, twist in and out together in a merry dance, culminating in that mad and terrible rush down the river which ends the mystery and the treasure. Dr. Doyle's admirers will read the little volume through eagerly enough, but they will hardly care to take it up again.

Although history has proved this judgment to be wide of the mark, the essential criticism that *The Sign of Four* is a mishmash of genres remains valid.

It was the idea of a series of short stories in the monthly magazine *The Strand* which changed literary history, though it remains unclear whether the idea was Doyle's own or that of the magazine's editor. Monthly magazines had been publishing serializations of novels throughout the Victorian era, but the disadvantage of this was that if a reader missed an episode it was very difficult to pick up the plot again. It was the idea of running a series of short stories in *The Strand Magazine* featuring the characters Holmes and Watson which made Holmes such a popular figure. The magazine-reading public liked the self-contained nature of each story combined with the continuity of characters from story to story.

Doyle's earnings for each of his first six stories for *The Strand* was £33 per story, for the next six it rose to £50, and for the next twelve to £83 (Cox 5). Still later, when Doyle's income from his writing gave him the financial security to do so, he made a determined attempt to end the public demand for Holmes stories. In "The Final Problem" (first published in *The Strand Magazine*, December 1893, and as the final story in *The Memoirs of Sherlock Holmes*, 1894) Holmes engages in a life-or-death struggle with his arch enemy and nemesis, the Napoleon of Crime, Professor James Moriarty. Both men apparently fall to their deaths at the Reichenbach Falls in Switzerland. The public was horrified. Doyle and Crowder report that "Over 20,000 people cancelled their subscriptions to *The Strand Magazine* in protest. Young men in London took to wearing black mourning bands. Some young women wore black" (58). One letter of protest from a female reader opened, "You Brute." To many of his readers, Holmes had become a *real* person.

Eventually, Doyle responded to public demand with the novel *The Hound of the Baskervilles*, a story set before Holmes' death. Generally regarded as the best of the Four Holmes novels, Doyle found that he had merely fueled the demand for more Holmes short stories, and so in "The Adventure of the Empty House" (1903) Holmes returns having spent the three years since his supposed death traveling the world, particularly Tibet and the mystic East. He explains to a relieved Watson that in the struggle he was able to use his knowledge of martial arts to send Moriarty to his death and that he then faked his own plunge over the falls in an effort to convince Moriarty's men, who would certainly seek to revenge the death of their leader, that he had also died.

From the title of the collection *His Last Bow*, it is clear that Doyle was making yet another attempt to wean his public away from Holmes, but one final collection, *The Case-Book of Sherlock Holmes*, was to follow. Of these stories Doyle and Crowder write, "The struggle Doyle had in sustaining the stories is evident; some of these adventures are a bit strained. But others are as good as anything he ever wrote" (24). The final Holmes story, "The Adventure of Shoscombe Old Place," first appeared in the *Strand Magazine* of April 1927.

The character of Sherlock Holmes was modeled in great part on Dr. Joseph Bell, Professor of Medicine at Edinburgh University, under whom Doyle studied. Doyle wrote that when Bell met patients:

> He would sit in his receiving room with a face like a Red Indian, and diagnose the people as they came in, before they even opened their mouths. He would tell them details of their past life; and

hardly would he ever make a mistake. (Quoted in Doyle and
 Crowder 32)
Holmes does the same thing both with Watson and with each new client.
However, there was also a great deal of the author himself in the character of
Holmes including prowess in boxing. In general, however, Doyle gave his
diagnostic thinking to Holmes and his love of physical activity to Watson, the
man of action and emotion: they are two aspects of their creator.

Dramatis Personae - List of Characters

The unprecedented popularity of Sherlock Holmes had a great deal to do with Doyle's mastery of the magazine series format, but it goes much deeper than that. Rosemary Jann argues convincingly that:

> Through the character of Holmes, Doyle brilliantly popularized the century's confidence in the uniform operation of scientific laws that allowed the trained observer to deduce causes from effects and what has passed from clues left behind. In the process he offered a powerful image of the scientist as hero, to counter the arrogance of the Victor Frankensteins and Dr. Jekylls of nineteenth-century fiction. (4)

To an age which had lost faith in the consolations of religion, Holmes would satisfy the desire of readers for "a transcendent moral order confirmed by justice and reason and for a society in which power naturally corresponds with virtue" (6). The days when criminals were romanticized, rather in the manner of Robin Hood, had long passed. To the literate middle classes, criminals were a threat to their own property and to the stability of a society which allowed them to make a reasonable living. Don Cox suggests Doyle provided the ideal hero to set before a crime-conscious middle class, which would, within six months of the appearance of *A Study in Scarlet* (December 1887), be reeling before the failure of the police to catch Jack the Ripper and temperamentally ready for a detective who could "foil every criminal" (34).

Sherlock Holmes:

Throughout the canon, Doyle gives hints about Holmes' early life and his family background, but it is unlikely that the author ever worked out a systematic biography for Holmes - rather he gives details as and when necessary with little concern for consistency. Certain conclusions can, however, be drawn. In "The Greek Interpreter," Holmes tells Watson, "'My ancestors were country squires, who appear to have led much the same life as is natural to their class.'" This places Holmes' forebears in the gentry class, rural landowners able to live off of the income generated either by leasing out their land for farming and/or by employing a manager to farm it. (Think of the Bennet family in *Pride and Prejudice*.)

On the evidence of his knowledge of Latin and other languages, Holmes clearly had the Classical education of a gentleman which means that he would have attended one of the public schools that existed to educate the male children of the upper middle classes. There is no mention either of which school or which university he attended (probably either London, Oxford or Cambridge), and it is unclear whether he graduated. To both his school and university, Holmes is indebted for his athletic prowess, particularly in fencing and boxing. Although he was, by his own admission, solitary and unsocial as a student, two former college friends, Victor Trevor and Reginald Musgrave, feature in his later investigations.

Having an inherited income of £400 a year, Holmes has no need to seek paid employment. Thus, in about 1876, after leaving university (with or without a degree), Holmes took rooms in Montague Street having, as he proudly boats to Dr. Watson, "'chosen my own particular profession, or rather created it, for I am the only one in the world [...] The only unofficial consulting detective.'" Over the next five years, Holmes spent his time studying criminology in the nearby British Museum Reading Room and developing his consultancy, in the process making a name for himself as an investigator with both the public and with Scotland Yard. The move to 221B Baker Street, sometime early in 1884, is an indication of his greater financial stability, though his need of someone with whom to share expenses shows that he was by no means wealthy. Although it has no relevance to *The Sign of Four*, Holmes does have an elder brother, Mycroft, whom he regards as intellectually his superior. Mycroft has some ill-defined position in government administration, though it is implied that he has a power and influence much beyond his actual title.

Forget any preconceptions you may have of Holmes as a middle-aged man wearing a deerstalker hat. (This image derives from original illustrations by Sidney Paget; Conan Doyle never describes Holmes as wearing one). At the time of *The Sign of Four*, Holmes, like his friend Watson, is in his mid- to late-twenties and very much at the height of his physical powers.

Here a word of warning is in order: almost from his first appearance in print, Holmes has seemed to many readers to be a real person - witness the thousands of letters written over decades to 221B Baker Street (a non-existent address) seeking the great detective's help. Many of those who write about Holmes do so as if Dr. Watson was the *real* author of the tales and Sir Arthur Conan Doyle merely his literary agent. In what has become an intellectual game (the first rule of which is that no one is ever to acknowledge that it *is* a game), these writers have great fun trying to reconcile the inconsistencies and fill in the gaps that they find in the Holmes canon. Such writing is not to be confused with literary criticism.

Dr. John H. Watson:

John Watson must also have been a product either of the public school system or perhaps of Blackheath Proprietary School (established in 1830 to give to boys whose parents could not afford to send them to a public schools a comparable education), for he reports himself as having played rugby for Blackheath Rugby Club. He took the degree Doctor of Medicine from London University in 1878 after which he studied at The Royal Victoria Military

Hospital at Netley in Hampshire. Upon completion of his course there (probably in 1880), he joined the Fifth Northumberland Fusiliers as an Assistant Surgeon stationed in India. These dates would make Holmes and Watson approximately the same age.

Having landed in Bombay, however, Watson and some fellow officers found that the regiment had already advanced into Afghanistan. Watson arrived in Candahar (Kandahar or Qandahar) to take part in the Second Anglo-Afghan War (1878 to 1880). After some short time, he was transferred to the Berkshires with which he was serving during the Battle of Maiwand (July 27th, 1880) in which two 2,500 British and Indian troops were defeated. British losses were: 21 officers and 948 soldiers killed, and 8 officers and 169 men wounded (britishbattles.com). Watson, who suffered a severe bullet wound, was carried from the field by his orderly and after a spell at the base hospital in Peshawur, a city in northwest Pakistan, during which his condition improved; he was evacuated to England on the troopship Orontes. He spent the next nine months as an invalid trying to improve his "irretrievably ruined" health.

Since he was unfit for military service, Watson retired on a pension of 11/6d (eleven shillings and six pence) a day. Having recovered somewhat, he came to London where he lived in a private hotel in the Strand, but soon found that his expenditures outran his income. He was introduced to Holmes by a mutual friend who knew that Holmes was looking for someone with whom to share the tenancy of rooms at 221B Baker Street. For both men the arrangement provided "'comfortable rooms at a reasonable price'" (*A Study in Scarlet*). Their first investigation, which Watson would eventually document under the title *A Study in Scarlet*, began on Tuesday, March 4th, 1884 with the delivery by hand of a letter from Inspector Tobias Gregson of Scotland Yard.

The details of Watson's wounds are confusing and inconsistent since on separate occasions he reports both that he was hit by a rifle bullet in the shoulder and in the leg. The severity of his wound also appears to vary: he returns to England with his health broken, but, though he is seen early in T*he Sign of Four* ruefully rubbing his aching leg, only a few hours later he is up for a six-mile walk. In *The Hound of the Baskervilles*, set a few years later, his ability to walk long distances in rugged Dartmoor suggests a full recovery!

Holmes is the stereotypical bachelor, but Watson has an eye for the ladies. In *The Sign of Four*, he speaks of himself as having had experience of women in "'many nations and three separate continents'" () which has led to inconclusive speculation about his travels prior to meeting Holmes. In *The Sign of Four* we hear of his proposed marriage to Mary Morstan which will cause him to vacate the Baker Street rooms (a clear indication, incidentally, that at this point Doyle did not envisage writing any more Holmes stories). There is every indication that his marriage was happy, although it lasted only about ten years. Watson would remain a widower until around 1912 when he must have re-married for Holmes reports, "the good Watson has deserted me for a wife, the only selfish action which I can recall in our association" ("The Blanched Soldier"). Clearly either Holmes' memory or Doyle's is here in error since this was Watson's *second* marriage and hence his second desertion of his friend. Following his marriage to Mary Morstan, Watson would set up a medical practice in Paddington which proved moderately successful, though he always seems both willing and able to hand his practice over to a locum whenever Holmes needs his help on a case.

Other Characters:

Spoiler alert! In giving a sketch of the characters in the novel, I have provided enough information to help the reader to understand how each fits into the plot. This inevitably means giving *some* details which explain the solution to the mystery.

Characters Connected to Holmes and Watson:

Mrs. Hudson: The landlady and housekeeper at 221B Baker Street who lives on the ground floor. She provides meals, cleaning services, and answers the door, showing visitors up to Holmes's rooms. Holmes is a difficult tenant: he is untidy, conducts smelly chemical experiments in his room, is visited by a constant succession of the oddest people, and occasionally fires his gun at the walls! Through all of this, Mrs. Hudson remains calm and caring. Her other tenants must exist but are never evident in the stories. (Booth identifies her model as the housekeeper, a "motherly woman," whom Doyle employed from December 1882 at his Portsmouth practice [95].).

The Baker Street Irregulars: A group of mainly homeless young boys (street Arabs) which Holmes uses occasionally when he needs to locate someone or something in London. Their 'commander' is "'My dirty little lieutenant, **Wiggins.**'"

Mr. Athelney Jones: An Inspector in the Metropolitan Police whose headquarters was Scotland Yard. Jones, like most of the other official policemen with whom Holmes' works, mocks his fanciful approach to solving crimes, but is not above making use of his expertise and taking credit for his successful resolution of baffling cases. Jones himself represents the worst aspects of the official police at this time: he is "the least-flattering portrait of a Scotland Yard detective in the canon" (Doyle and Crowder 113), and this is the only Holmes story in which he appears. **Toby:** A mongrel dog with an amazingly sensitive nose for following a scent which Holmes borrows from his owner, **Mr. Sherman**, to track the murderers.

The Morstan Family and Connections:

Captain Arthur Morstan: An officer in the British Indian Army who served in the 34th Bombay Infantry. He returned from India in December 1878 and arranged to meet his daughter, Mary, at the Langham Hotel in London. However, although he had checked into the hotel, he did not keep this appointment and was never seen again.

Mary Morstan: Holmes's client. She is a young Englishwoman, born in India but raised in Scotland, whose widowed father disappeared ten years previously. Since then, beginning in 1882, she has for the last six years received annually a single pearl of great value delivered anonymously. On the day she consults Holmes, she has received an anonymous letter describing her as "'a wronged woman'" and requesting her to go to the Lyceum Theater that evening with two friends.

Mrs. Cecil Forrester: This lady employs Miss Morstan's as a governess but shows her genuine concern and friendship. It is she who suggests that Mary should consult Holmes because he once helped her with "a little domestic complication."

The Sholto Family and Connections:

Major John Sholto: Formerly an officer in the 34th Bombay Infantry, the same regiment as Captain Morstan with whom he was on excellent terms. Having apparently inherited a considerable fortune, he retired from the Army, returned to England, and purchased Pondicherry Lodge in Upper Norwood where he was living at the time of Morstan's disappearance. However, when contacted by Mary, he claimed to have no knowledge that his former friend had returned to England. Before he died, on the 28th of April, 1882, he revealed to his twin sons that Morstan died accidentally as they argued over some treasure that had been handed over to them for transportation from India to England. He dies before he can reveal the hiding place of the treasure to his sons. All that he gives them is some jewelry, including a number of fine pearls.

Lal Chowdar - Indian servant who is totally loyal to Major Sholto. He has died before the start of the story.

Bartholomew Sholto: On his father's death, he continues to live at Pondicherry Lodge in Upper Norwood. He and his brother search every part of the house and gardens for the missing treasure mentioned by their dying father. The day after having located the jewels in the attic space at Pondicherry Lodge, he is found murdered in his locked room.

Thaddeus Sholto: On his father's death, he moves out of Pondicherry Lodge, though why he does so is never made clear. Feeling a moral obligation to share his wealth with Mary Morstan, it is he who sends her a single pearl each year. When he learns that his brother has located the full treasure, he contacts Mary Morstan because he feels that she should receive her father's share.

Williams: Loyal servant of Thaddeus Sholto. Originally employed by Major John Sholto as a bodyguard, he is an ex-boxer who was once light-weight champion of England.

McMurdo: Loyal servant of Bartholomew Sholto. Originally employed by

Major John Sholto as a bodyguard, he is an ex-boxer at whose benefit Holmes accepted the challenge to box him in an exhibition bout.

Lal Rao: Indian butler in the employ first of Major and then of Bartholomew Sholto.

Mrs. Bernstone: Housekeeper in the employ first of Major and then of Bartholomew Sholto.

The Four:

Jonathan Small: A former soldier in the Army of India who had known Major Sholto and Captain Morstan in the Andaman Islands. Small lost a leg when he was attacked by a crocodile. Small and one accomplice seek to regain the treasure, committing murder in doing so.

Mahomet Singh and Abdullah Khan: Two Punjabi Sikhs assigned, under the command of Small, to guard one of the doors to Agra Fort during the Indian Mutiny.

Dost Akbar: A Punjabi Sikh who is the foster-brother of Abdullah Khan.

Other Characters in India:

John Holder: Company sergeant in Small's Indian regiment who saved his life following a crocodile attack.

Abelwhite: An indigo-planter who employed Small after his accident as an overseer on his Indian plantation.

Dawson: Abelwhite's accountant and manager. He and his wife become early victims of the Indian Mutiny.

Achmet: Disguised as an Indian merchant, he is the servant who is entrusted with half of the rajah's treasure during the Indian Mutiny.

Other Characters in the Andaman Islands:

Dr. Somerton: British surgeon from whom Small learned something about dispensing drugs.

Lieutenant Bromley Brown: One of three officers (Morstan and Sholto being the others) in command of native troops on Blair Island in the Andaman Islands.

Tonga: A native of the Islands and a devoted follower of Jonathan Small.

Other Characters in London:

Mordecai Smith: A boat keeper who rents and drives boats on the Thames. He is engaged by Jonathan Small to have the *Aurora*, a fast steam launch, ready for their get-away. Small pays him well but tells him nothing of the crime in which he is an unwitting accomplice.

Mrs. Smith: Mordecai's wife who tells Holmes about her husband's absence enabling him to connect Smith's boat with Small's escape.

Jim Smith: Smith's oldest son who is on the *Aurora* with his father.

The Sign of Four by Sir Arthur Conan Doyle

Historical Background:

When Doyle wrote *The Sign of Four*, the historical references which are essential to understanding the mystery would have been fresh in the minds of his readers. Modern readers, however, need some assistance.

The East India Company - A Brief Timeline:

1600 - Founded by Royal Charter of Elizabeth I, the Honourable East India Company (HEIC) was a private company established to trade with the Far East. Shares were owned by wealthy individuals but the Crown held no shares, and thus the administration of the Company was virtually autonomous.

1757 - Following the defeat of Indian and French forces at the Battle of Plassey, the Company established itself as the ruling power in most of India.

1857 to 1858 - The Indian Mutiny. (See below)

August 2nd, 1858 - The British Parliament passed a bill for the transfer of control of the Government of India from the East India Company to the Crown. The East India Company was defunct.

The Indian Mutiny of 1857 to 1858 - A Brief Timeline:

February 26th to May 9th, 1857:
Unrest, refusal to perform rifle practice, and mutiny by sepoys of the 19th and 34th Native Infantry, and the 3rd Bengal Light Cavalry. Harsh punishments by British officers inflamed the situation.

May 10th & 11th, 1857:
Mutiny of sepoys at Meerut. The mutineers headed for Delhi, and in both Meerut and Delhi, Europeans and Christians were massacred.

May 12th to July 7th, 1857:
The rebellion spread rapidly, and the Indian rebels gained control of key cities. A number of senior British generals died leaving the Army with a lack of leadership. On June 30th, following the British defeat at Chinhat, Indians besieged the remnant of British forces in the Lucknow Residency.

July 12th to August 16th 1857:
Brigadier-General Sir Henry Havelock won a series of victories at and near Cawnpore. The tide of the rebellion appeared to have turned.

August 17th, 1857, to June 11th, 1858:
Battles gave victories to both sides, but the momentum remained with the British:

September 10th - The re-capture of Delhi;

November 14th to 19th - The relief of Lucknow allowed the women and children to be evacuated;

December 6th - Having lost the Second Battle of Cawnpore, the British won the decisive Third Battle of Cawnpore;

March 21st - The rebels were finally driven from Lucknow.

June 12th to 19th, 1858:
British victories in battles at Nawabganj, Kotah-ki-Serai, and Gwalior effectively ended The Indian Mutiny.

August 2nd, 1858:
Queen Victoria approved a Parliamentary Bill that transferred the administration of India from the East India Company to the Crown.

The Andaman Island Prison - A Brief Timeline:

1789-96: The English government of Bengal established a prison colony first at Port Blair and then at Port Cornwallis, but abandoned the Andaman Islands because of the unhealthy climate and the hostility of the native islanders.

November 1857: Originally planned for 1855, but delayed by the Indian Mutiny, work began on a new penal colony at Port Blair. The prison housed mainly political prisoners, that is, Indians who opposed British rule. Mortality amongst the inmates was very high.

1910: The famous Cellular Prison was completed at Port Blair. It had 698 cells in which prisoners were kept in solitary confinement. It is often mistakenly assumed that this is the prison referred to in the novel, but the Cellular Prison post-dates the period in which the action on the Andaman Islands is set by over thirty years.

The Sign of Four by Sir Arthur Conan Doyle

Chapter I: The Science of Deduction

Questions:

1. In the opening paragraph, how does Doyle make dramatic the description of Holmes injecting himself?

2. List the reasons that Watson gives Holmes for his wanting to stop (or at least to limit) his friend's taking of drugs, and then list the reasons that Watson gives the reader to explain why he has, until this moment, taken no action.

3. What defense of his use of these substances does Holmes make? (Consider his two speeches, "'Perhaps you are...'" and "'My mind...'")

4. What, for Holmes, is the attraction of criminal investigation?

5. How would you describe Holmes' attitude to official policemen?

6. Explain the difference between an "'unofficial detective?'" and "'unofficial *consulting* detective'" (emphasis added).

7. What exactly is it about Watson's account of the Jefferson Hope case to which Holmes objects? Why is Watson so annoyed by Holmes' criticism of his work?

8. In two columns, make a list of Francois Le Villard's qualities and his shortcomings as a detective according to Holmes' assessment.

9. Holmes' examples of the application of science to detection strike the modern reader as rather obvious, if not primitive, but they were revolutionary in their day. The obvious omission is fingerprinting. Research the use of fingerprints in criminal detections. When was a reliable method of 'lifting' fingerprints from objects discovered? When did police begin to use fingerprints to identify people and to catch criminals? When and where was a database of finger prints first established?

10. In describing Holmes' deductions about Watson's visit to the Post Office, Doyle cheats a little. There are, in fact, many other things that Watson might have been doing in a Post Office other than sending a telegram - Doyle just hopes that the reader will be so impressed that we will not think of them. Name three other things for which Watson might equally have visited the Post Office.

11. The watch that Watson hands over is a pocket (not a wrist) watch, that is, a watch on a chain kept in the pocket of the user's waistcoat. Make a list of the kinds of evidence Holmes is likely to look for on such a watch.

12. Make a list of the conclusions which Holmes has drawn from the watch and for each one suggest what it is that he might have noticed about the watch which could have led to this conclusion. (Like Watson, you will probably find it "simplicity itself" when Holmes explains it!)

13. What does Holmes acknowledge to be the limitation of deductions based on observation?

Commentary:

Since *The Sign of Four* (1890) was only the second Sherlock Holmes story, being published three years after *A Study in Scarlet* (1887), Doyle feels the need to reintroduce the two main characters and to set out once again the principles and practice of scientific detection. This section establishes Holmes' European-wide reputation amongst members of the official police and gives more information on the methods he uses in his investigations, methods which the police (by implication) do not use. However, Doyle runs into some problems here. Is it really believable that, in the year since its publication, Watson has never mentioned *A Study in Scarlet* to his friend? Is it credible that Watson, who has been living for four years with Holmes, should need to be reminded that his friend is the world's first consulting detective, or that he should not know that Holmes has written several books. The books are, after all, in clear sight in the sitting room! (Once Doyle discovered the short story format for Holmes' cases, he would fill those four years with investigations, but at the time he wrote *The Sign of Four* he had no thought of doing so.)

One of the most original aspects of Doyle's novel is that the protagonist, Holmes, is far from likeable, at least not on first acquaintance. He comes across as arrogant, condescending, aloof, and totally self-centered. Nowhere is this more obvious than in his refusal to accept Watson's objective analysis of his own drug habit and its inevitable consequences for his mental and physical health. Ironically, Watson uses the same observational and logical approach that Holmes applies to crime. One wonders why, apart from his obviously superior intellectual powers, Watson puts up with him for a moment. As you read the novel, be on the lookout for those admirable qualities which Watson (and ultimately the reader) finds in his friend.

Almost all of the Sherlock Holmes stories, whether novels or short stories, begin with a demonstration of Holmes' powers of observation and of deduction from that observation. Often, as here, the subject is Watson, but it is also frequently the client about whom Holmes is able to deduce a great deal. Sometimes it is both. On these occasions, Watson and/or the client is always initially baffled by Holmes' deductions, but ends up commenting that it is really simple - which it is, once Holmes has explained it.

In his deductions about Watson sending a telegram and concerning the previous owner of Watson's watch, the reader sees the brilliance of Holmes as observer and logical thinker. Holmes observes "'a little reddish mould [soil] adhering'" from which he deduces that his friend must have gone to the Seymour Street Post Office to send a telegram: the amazed, and baffled, Watson confirms the truth of this conclusion. Passing rapidly over the unlikely detail of Seymour Street uniquely having "'earth of this peculiar reddish tint,'" and the fact that Watson might simply have been walking past the post office on (which was no great distance from Baker Street) to go somewhere else, Holmes ignores other reasons why Watson might have gone to the Post Office. Perhaps he went to collect a parcel, or to buy a postal order, or to make an enquiry. Doyle typically discourages the reader from seeing the holes in Holmes' reasoning by ensuring that is right.

The second demonstration of Holmes' skills is equally impressive. Holmes is able correctly to identify the owner of the watch and to describe the man's character. Some of his reasoning, for example from the initials engraved on the watch, is water-tight, but some is not. Holmes observes "'thousands of scratches all around the hole-marks where he key has slipped,'" and from this he concludes that Watson's brother was habitually drunk since "'you will never see a drunkard's watch without [such scratches].'" There are, however, plenty of other explanations. Perhaps the brother suffered from a disease which made his hand unsteady, such as Parkinson's; perhaps he was in the habit of winding his watch in the dark; or perhaps he was simply as careless in winding his watch as he was in his general use of the watch whose case is dented and scratched. Of course, the reader does not have the watch in front of him/her, which makes Holmes' deduction even more impressive. We also, however, see his limitations as a human being, for he gets so carried away with his analysis of what the watch tells him about its owner that he does not realize the human context in which he is stating his conclusions and says things which are very hurtful to Watson. To Holmes' credit, when this is drawn to his attention he acknowledges his fault and is very apologetic: we begin to see why Watson remains his friend.

Watson changes the subject rather abruptly to ask if Holmes is working on a case, and when he learns that his friend is at his wits end for lack of a challenge the housekeeper conveniently announces the arrival of a client. This sort of thing happens all of the time at Baker Street - it is not great writing, but it certainly moves the plot along. The story begins on July 8th, 1888.

Chapter II: The Statement of the Case

Questions:

1. What conclusions does Watson come to about the circumstances and character of Miss Morstan from his observation of her?

2. Why do you think that Watson twice offers to leave the room? Explain why first Holmes and then Miss Morstan indicate that they each desire him to remain.

3. How old would Miss Morstan have been at the time her father disappeared? How old would she be at the time of her visit to Holmes?

4. Why would someone send Miss Morstan a pearl every year? Who might that person be? Make a list of possible answers.

5. Why do you think that Holmes asks, "'Has anything else occurred to you?'"? (Clue: The story begins, we soon learn, on July 8th. When was the last time that she was sent a pearl?)

6. How might Holmes spend the two-and-a-half hours until Miss Morstan's return looking into her case? What would you do? (Clue: What would be the equivalent in Holmes day to looking up the case on the Internet?)

7. How does Holmes justify his lack of concern for the attractiveness, or otherwise, of his clients?

8. How is Holmes' recommendation of Reade's book consistent with his approach to criminal investigations?

9. For what reasons does Watson suppress his romantic thoughts about Miss Morstan?

Commentary:

Miss Morstan is the stereotypical 'damsel in distress' in need of a knight. She appears innocent, friendly, and thoughtful. These qualities attract Watson, but Holmes becomes interested only when she tells him, "'I can hardly imagine anything more strange, more utterly inexplicable, than the situation in which I find myself.'" This puzzle offers a stimulation superior even to that of cocaine.

The disappearance of Captain Morstan is strange, but not in itself particularly interesting as a puzzle - people disappear all of the time, usually for the most mundane of reasons. It is the sending of the six pearls which seems inexplicable. The mysterious letter gives the investigation some urgency. The anonymous writer appoints a time when the public will be gathering outside the theater for the evening performance, which suggests that this person has no malevolent intention. The idea that Miss Morstan is a "wronged woman" once

The Sign of Four by Sir Arthur Conan Doyle

again presents her as an innocent victim of forces beyond her knowledge. Presumably, she has been swindled out of an inheritance of some kind since there is no indication that she has been wronged in any other way.

The mysterious letter gives the investigation some urgency. The anonymous writer appoints a time when the public will be gathering outside the theater for the evening performance, which suggests that this person has no malevolent intention. The idea that Miss Morstan is a "wronged woman" once again presents her as an innocent victim of forces beyond her knowledge. Presumably, she has been swindled out of an inheritance of some kind since there is no indication that she has been wronged in any other way.

A postmark is a marking in ink made on a letter, package, or postcard showing the time and date that the item was first received by the postal service. This mark is usually alongside the ink marks which cover the stamps to ensure that they cannot be reused. Given that at this date most mail was delivered either the same day or the following day, it is likely that the story begins on July 8th, which makes Watson's statement in the next chapter that "It was a September evening ..." inexplicable. Apparently Doyle spotted the inconsistency and wrote to the editor of Lippincott's Monthly Magazine on March 6th, 1890, that it needed to be corrected. Why it never has been is not clear.

Names are important in fiction. The name 'Mary' associates Miss Morstan with the Virgin Mary and therefore with purity. The name 'Major Sholto' is unusual since Sholto is not normally a family name. Given its lack of familiarity and its rather unpleasant sound, it sets up negative expectations in the reader.

The reader now discovers that Watson is as attracted to Miss Morstan as it has been obvious that she has been attracted to him. The reaction of the two men to the attractive client shows another aspect of their very different characters. Holmes' claim not to have noticed the attractive appearance of Miss Morstan seems like a pose to make gentle fun of his gullible friend Watson. No doubt the supreme detective has recognized signs of Watson's attraction to the young lady.

Even today, handwriting analysis is an imprecise science, but the deductions that Holmes makes from the anonymous handwriting seem particularly arbitrary and unconvincing. Notice that they depend upon massive generalizations (stereotypes) about the nature and conduct of people based on identifying particular characteristics.

Holmes already has a plan of investigation in mind and begins immediately.

Chapter III: In Quest of a Solution

Questions:

1. Using the dates that Holmes gives here and those which have already been given, construct a timeline beginning at 1860, the approximate date of Mary Morstan's birth and ending on July 8th, 1888, the probable date at this point in the story. Be prepared to add to the timeline (at either end) as the plot develops.

2. Holmes suggests, but does not clearly state, the 'theory of the crime' which he has developed. In scientific terms, this is his hypothesis; further testing will be needed to give it the status of a theory (compare the Theory of Evolution). State the narrative of the crime which Holmes has developed

3. Holmes' description of the diagram on the paper is precise. Following it carefully, draw the diagram. (Feel free to use your imagination to 'fill out' the details.)

4. How does Doyle establish a setting appropriate to the action in his description of the approach of the carriage to the Lyceum Theater?

5. Even if Holmes does not immediately see that the paper which Miss Morstan hands him is a vital clue (and I think that he does), the reader must surely understand it as such. (Otherwise why would Doyle have included it?) Explain how you think that it may change the hypothesis of the crime.

6. What clues are we given to the eventual marriage of Watson and Miss Morstan ?

7. Comment on the effect of the word "'it'" in the final paragraph.

Commentary

Holmes returns feeling typically pleased with himself - the man is insufferably arrogant at times! He suggests a narrative which covers the facts he has discovered, though not (as Watson points out) the six pearls and the promise to right the wrongs done to Miss Morstan. However, Holmes is confident that Watson will have no alternative theory to offer, and he is right. (Technically, at this stage, Holmes' has developed an hypothesis. See below.)

Holmes very quickly discovers that the case will be more complex than he first supposed. He is being honest when he says, "'No, I confess that I do not see how this bears upon the matter,'" for he spends the remainder of the journey in silent thought. He is, however, quick to admit that he may have underestimated the complexity of the case, which is refreshing.

Interestingly, the coachman is willing to take Miss Morstan's word that her companions are not policemen - a lady of her social class would never lie. The assertive manner of the coachman, the speed at which he drives, and his deliberate attempt to confuse his passengers as to their route all add to the excitement. However, it is by no means clear why the coachman takes such a circuitous route. Since no attempt is made to keep the address to which they are driven a secret, it must be to shake off anyone who might be following Miss Morstan. Contrast Holmes' calm with the anxious concern shared by Watson and Miss Morstan. Watson, not being a native of the city, does not know London particularly well, whilst Holmes knows it intimately. Doyle, however, only moved to London in the early 1890s and so was not particularly familiar with the huge city. Most of the roads mentioned actually existed, though a few were outdated. It is certainly possible to trace the general route of the carriage, but once again Doyle aimed for impact rather than absolute accuracy. It has been suggested that he used a slightly outdated map of London in describing the route.

In a world where most of Doyle's readers had never been out of Britain, foreign places were much more mysterious and exotic than they seem today. This was particularly true of the Mystic East, a place of mysterious religions, rituals, and magic. Doyle plays on this stereotype to titillate the reader's interest.

Chapter IV: The Story of the Bald-Headed Man

Questions:

1. Who might this bald-headed man be? (Take account of his age, which is thirty, and compare this with the timeline you have constructed.)

2. Speculate on the identity and character of "Brother Bartholomew." It is now clear why Miss Morstan was instructed to bring *two* friends. Explain.

3. You should have no real difficulty explaining just why "Brother Bartholomew" is so very angry with Mr. Sholto's actions. Explain.

4. Major John Sholto came back from the East with "a considerable sum of money, a large collection of valuable curiosities." Why is this suspicious?

5. Why is the character Jonathan Small important to an understanding Major John Sholto's story?

6. Who might have written the letter that Major John Sholto received and which frightened him so badly? What do you think it said? (Note: Neither question is definitively answered in the novel.)

7. What do you think that the Agar treasure might be and where might John Sholto have hidden it?

8. What is the significance of the brothers finding "a single footmark" in the soil beneath the window?

9. The reader now has a number of unanswered questions which function to motivate reading on. Make a list of the things that you *need* to know in order to understand this mystery better.

10. What do you think will happen when Thaddeus Sholto confronts his brother?

11. Why is Watson so down-cast when he learns the value of the treasure?

Commentary:

The description of the man responsible for Miss Morstan having been brought to his house is exotic and grotesque. Jennifer Fraser comments that "Watson's description of Thaddeus Sholto's apartment demonstrates the Western tendency to associate foreign objects with decadence." He is the first of several examples in the novel of the malicious debilitating, even criminalizing, impact of contact with India. Doyle is catering to the reading public's love of mystery and sensationalism. Certainly Sholto is ugly; his physical state may be the result of drug use. His identity remains a mystery for long enough to stimulate the

The Sign of Four by Sir Arthur Conan Doyle

reader's interest.

Amongst Mr. Thaddeus Sholto's many idiosyncrasies is his hypochondria (that is, his constant fear of being ill). Illness would not be surprising since he obviously lives a sedentary and unhealthy life. It is, however, surprising that Watson, who is not currently a practicing doctor, should be carrying around his stethoscope (presumably in his doctor's bag) just on the off-chance that he might need it. Either Watson was a very dedicated doctor, or Doyle once again does not let probability get in the way of a good story.

Miss Morstan learns for the first time that her father is dead, though given that he disappeared so mysteriously ten years previously, she must have prepared herself for such a revelation. Thaddeus Sholto implies that Captain Morstan died of a heart attack.

The reader is not longer left in any doubt that Watson has fallen for Miss Morstan. When a man as mild-mannered at Watson feels the urge to hit another man across the face for causing Miss Morstan emotional pain, we can conclude that he is in love. Miss Mary Morstan proves herself a woman with spirit: she is the first to tire of Mr. Sholto rambling about his art collection and to insist that he come to the point. Watson supports her by suggesting that if they have to travel to Norwood they should get started. Holmes is uncharacteristically silent.

As you read Major John Sholto's narrative as it is given by his son, remember one other character already mentioned in the story: Jonathan Small. Notice how cleverly Doyle has Thaddeus Sholto state that his father told him "'the fate of Arthur Morstan'" and then he delays the moment when he tells the reader what happened. Thaddeus' statement that his father "'lived in great luxury'" is at odds with John Sholto's claim not to have "'made use of'" the treasure he brought from India but to have hoarded it like a miser. Anyway, this establishes that Miss Morstan's full share of the treasure is largely intact.

The death-bed confession, the mention of hidden treasure, and the appearance of a face at the window are all rather conventional elements of the Gothic horror genre, but Doyle certainly makes them work. He knows that he is writing in a tradition and that his readers have certain expectations which he is happy to fulfill.

The mystery of the six pearls received annually by Miss Morstan is now explained and we begin to understand the difference in temperament between Mr. Thaddeus Sholto and his brother Bartholomew. It becomes clear why Thaddeus Sholto suggested that Miss Morstan should bring *two* friends with her to meet him. Clearly he wants to be sure of outnumbering his brother by three to one because he anticipates Bartholomew objecting to the idea of sharing the treasure.

The method used to locate the hiding place of the treasure is worthy of Holmes himself in that it is logical and analytical. However, it is hard to believe that it would have taken the brothers six full years to discover the location of the treasure which they knew to be in either the house or grounds of Pondicherry Lodge. Finally we learn that this is a very high stakes game. The treasure is worth a king's ransom. However, it appears not to have occurred to anyone (with the probable exception of Holmes) that such a great treasure could not have legally come into the hands of British Army officers.

Chapter V: The Tragedy of Pondicherry Lodge

Questions:

1. What has happened to Bartholomew Sholto?

2. What do you imagine that Mrs. Bernstone and Holmes are supposed to have seen through the keyhole in the door?

3. What is "the Sign of the Four"? Who are the Four and what is their connection to the treasure that Major Sholto brought back to England? (Clue: Speculate.)

Commentary:

The title of this chapter acts as a hook since it promises excitement.

The stone wall around the Lodge makes it sound like a miniature fortress, although as we have already seen an intruder, with a wooden leg, was able to get into and out of the grounds with relative ease.

The unusual behavior of Bartholomew during the day and the fact that he is not awake to greet his brother (whose visit he is expecting) are ominous. The reader anticipates that he may be dead.

Holmes' boxing skills figure in several of the stories. We normally think of Holmes as middle-aged, but this is one of the earliest stories, so at the time of the contest he would be in his early-twenties.

The love between Watson and Miss Morstan becomes clear at this point, as does their future life together.

Pondicherry Lodge obviously has extensive grounds, though these cannot be more than an acre or two since the house is in the suburbs not in the countryside proper.

The door to Bartholomew's room is fitted with a mortise lock. The key is in the lock on the inside, but it has been turned to secure the door leaving the lower part of the key-hole opening unobstructed.

Both Mrs. Bernstone and Holmes look through the key hole of Bartholomew's door. The housekeeper reports that she "never saw him with such a face on him as that" and Holmes sees something which he calls "'devilish,'" and which Watson says made him "more moved than I had ever before seen him." This is quite remarkable since both Mrs. Bernstone and Holmes look through a keyhole, at night, into a room which has no light. How they could see *anything* so clearly is hard to explain. That the key-hole should align exactly with the body of Bartholomew is hard to believe.

The reference to moonlight is a belated attempt to explain how Mrs. Bernstone and Holmes could see into the room, but that Watson could distinguish red hair by moonlight stretches credulity once more.

Why Bartholomew should have set up a chemical laboratory in his bedroom when he has the entire house is never explained. Why he should have wanted a chemical laboratory at all is a complete mystery, similarly what possible use he could have for a large supply of creosote. The reader might suspect that the idea of the chemicals is simply a device to allow one of the intruders to step into something which has a strong scent.

Holmes tells an entirely bemused Watson, "'I only require a few missing links to have an entirely connected case.'" Doyle hopes that the reader will be as confused by all of these remarkable events as is the good doctor. Here the reader not only learns that there *is* a solution to the puzzle but that Holmes is very close to having solved it. This acts as another hook to make us want to read on.

Chapter VI: Sherlock Holmes Gives a Demonstration

Questions:

1. Put simply, how did the man with a wooden leg get into the locked room of Bartholomew Sholto and then get out again leaving the window and door locked from the inside? An annotated diagram might be the best way to illustrate this.

2. "'Holmes,' I said, in a whisper, 'a child has done the horrid thing.'" Although you do not have the advantage of Holmes' knowledge, can you suggest a more logical explanation?

3. How, precisely was Bartholomew murdered?

4. Make a list of the errors which Jones makes in his investigation. Keep going with that list of Jones' mistakes to the end of the chapter.

5. From where does Holmes get the name Jonathan Small? How does he come to attach it to the intruder who has a wooden lag?

6. Some of the things that Holmes deduces about Small are obvious, like the wooden leg, but how does he know that the man is "a middle-aged man, much sunburned, and has been a convict"?

Commentary:

The reader will notice that Miss Morstan had been completely forgotten by Holmes, Watson, and Sholto. Having been conveniently got out of the way by the author, Doyle offers a belated explanation, "Miss Morstan had remained behind with the frightened housekeeper." At times in an adventure story such as this, female characters become simply surplus to requirements! Holmes sends Sholto off to inform the police without making any reference to her, and while he and Watson (who is supposed to be in love with her) spend thirty minutes examining the scene of the crime neither of them gives a single thought about her.

The 'locked room mystery' is something like the holy grail of crime fiction: a man (or woman) is found to have been violently murdered in a room the door(s) and window(s) of which are securely locked from the inside. In this case, the door to Bartholomew Sholto's room is locked from the inside, and the key is still in the lock. The door is also secured by an internal bolt. The windows have been secured from the inside. This poses the questions: How did the murderer get in? and: How did the murderer get out?

Here we see Holmes' methods of observation and deduction at the scene of the crime. Although the explanation of how the murderer and the thief gained access to a locked room is amazing, Holmes is able to deduce the truth through observation, knowledge, and pure logic. The remaining questions are: How did the rope get into the room? How did the hook come to be in the wall? How did there come to be a trap door leading into and out of an enclosed roof space? Only one of these questions is ever answered in the novel.

The garret room which Holmes and Watson discover is hardly the 'secret room' earlier described by Thaddeus Sholto. It may indeed be bigger than expected, but there is always a space in a house with a pitched room between the ceiling of the top floor and the roof itself. Based on Bartholomew's calculations, the "little garret" would have been only four feet taller than one would have expected - hardly enough for a separate hidden room. Surely it would not take six years and complex measuring to suggest the idea of looking for the treasure in the loft!

The question of the child-murderer is dropped for a moment. Knowing that he has only a few moments to examine the scene of the crime before the police arrive and begin walking all over it, Holmes quickly examines it without expecting to find anything. Quite why he does all that measuring is unexplained. He does discover that the diminutive person (Number One) who let the man with the wooden leg (Number Two) into the window stepped in some spilled creosote. To call this "'luck'" is something of an understatement! Presumably Doyle found no other way in which even Holmes' analytical powers could trace the murderers.

The police, in the person of Inspector Jones, are portrayed as comic figures: big, loud, arrogantly self-confident, and (quite honestly) stupid. To watch Jones go to work on the case is to see, by way of contrast, the skills of Holmes. Inspector Jones is that most dangerous combination - a foolish man who is convinced of his own wisdom. He jumps to conclusions and then fits the evidence to match his hypothesis rather than using it to test and to refine that hypothesis.

Holmes' theory of the crime, thus far, is that the intruder had an accomplice who entered through the trapdoor in the roof, killed Bartholomew with a blowpipe, and then threw down a rope from the window by which he was able to get up to and later down from the room. The accomplice exited from the roof. Here are a few unanswered questions:

- Why was Bartholomew storing corrosive liquids in his room? How and when did the carboy containing creosote crack?
- Why was there "a trapdoor which leads out onto the roof" when all access to the garret had been covered over and hidden? What was its original purpose?
- Where did the rope come from? If it was already in Bartholomew's room, that was a tremendous piece of luck! What on earth was it doing there? If it was not, how was it carried there by Number One? Remember that the rope must be sixty feet long.

- Why is there a "great hook in the wall" of Bartholomew's room? If it was already in Bartholomew's room, that was another tremendous piece of luck! What was its original purpose? Or was it brought by Number One?
- Why did Number One leave the rope in the room since it provided clear evidence of how the crime was committed? Why not just throw it down to the one-legged man after he had climbed down it to make his escape?
- How can it be that no one in the house heard or saw two men (one hampered by a wooden leg) climbing up and down the outside of the building and searching Sholto's room?
- Since it would have been impossible for anyone to have climbed up to the window in Bartholomew's room, how is it that the roof (at least sixty feet from the ground) was accessible? How did Number One climb up to it? How did he get down? Remember that he is a very small person which would not make climbing any easier.
- Some of these questions will be answered in the narrative, and some will not.

Holmes tells Watson, "'This unexpected occurrence ... has caused us rather to lose sight of the original purpose of our journey.'" This is something of an understatement since Miss Morstan has been left with the housekeeper for almost an hour. The fact is that Doyle simply has to get her out of the way so that Holmes can examine the scene of the crime and he does it in a perfunctory manner.

Chapter VII: The Episode of the Barrel

Questions:

1. Precisely why is Dr. Watson unable to show his concern and affection for Miss Morstan on their drive back to her home?

2. What do you think will prove to be distinctive about the footprints? (This is not such an impossible question as it might appear. Remember that the origin of this mystery goes back to India and the Andaman Islands. Think of the footprints of a native of this part of the world.)

3. Holmes is just about to set out his theory of the crime, so you should try to do the same. You need to begin by explaining how the treasure came into the possession of Major Sholto.

4. It is not clear from Holmes' scenario who was the author of the letter which Major Sholto received telling him of the escape of one, or more, of the original signers of the treasure map. Was it written by Captain Morstan or by Jonathan Small himself or by someone else? Justify your answer.

5. Holmes says of Jonathan Small, "'He bore no grudge against Bartholomew Sholto.'" Explain why this is so.

6. Why do you think that Doyle is so precise in his description of the route taken by Holmes and Watson? Why not just make up the names of the roads?

7. Why do Holmes and Watson burst out laughing?

8. What would you predict to be Holmes' next move? Explain.

Commentary:

Here are three examples of Watson's usefulness to the narrative. Firstly, Watson only meets Miss Morstan at 6 p.m. and since it is now 2 a.m. he has known her precisely eight hours for much of which time he has not been in her presence. This example of love at first sight allows the author to introduce romance into his story. Secondly, at this point, Doyle considerately employs Watson to reprise the story so far, just to make sure that the reader has not forgotten some salient point. Thirdly, Watson is given the practical tasks of returning Miss Morstan to her home and fetching the tracker dog, allowing Holmes to continue his investigation. Mr. Sherman's shop seems like something out of Charles Dickens, perhaps the Old Curiosity Shop. Doyle continues to give this story the flavor of a Gothic novel, full of the mysterious and the grotesque.

Holmes takes some risk to confirm that it was possible to climb up to and down from the roof by using the water pipe. This explanation is hardly convincing, however, since Holmes has a lantern with him and is only climbing down. The culprit climbed up in the dark carrying, amongst other things, a sixty foot rope.

Watson's affirmative answer to his question, "'Are you game for a six-mile trudge, Watson?'" seems to indicate a wonderful recovery in his injury since lunch the previous day when he sat "nursing [his] wounded leg." Additionally, Holmes could not possibly have known how far the trail which Toby is going to follow would lead them. For all he knew, the murderer could have lived next door!

We see Holmes' vanity in his defense of using Toby to track the murderers; he would not want Watson to think that solving the crime was a matter of good fortune (one of the criminals stepping in creosote). The problem has ceased to be an intellectual puzzle and Holmes lament this turn of events. Toby has just been described as starting off "at a pace which strained his leash and kept us at the top of our speed." How Holmes finds the breath to give the long explanation, and how he collects his thoughts whilst still keeping up with the hound on the scent is remarkable! Here is Holmes at his brilliant (or most infuriating) best, laying out an entire theory of the crime based upon his deductions to an awe-struck Watson.

Holmes says of the Sholto butler, Lal Rao that "Mrs. Bernstone gives him far from a good character." This must be another example of inherent racism: Doyle takes the word of the English Mrs. Bernstone over that of the Indian servant without question. Since it is now clear that the key to this mystery lies in the past history of those involved in India and the Andaman Islands, this seems to be a good place to alert the reader to look out for the way in which 'people of color' are presented in the novel. This commentary will be highly critical of Doyle's resort to the negative racist stereotypes that were common in his day because it is bad writing which panders to the thirst in readers for the exotic and the sensational. However, in fairness, Conan Doyle was both in life and sometimes in his writing more enlightened. Doyle and Crowder point out that in 1907 Conan Doyle worked tirelessly to prove the innocence of George Edalji, a Parsee Indian accused of mutilating animals because, "He was convinced that Edalji was innocent and that racial prejudice had played a part in his conviction" (64). The same authors comment that in the story "The Yellow Face" Conan Doyle "has Holmes display a positively enlightened attitude to interracial marriage" (73).

The route which Holmes and Watson follow takes them to the South Bank of the River Thames perhaps half a mile to the west of Vauxhall Bridge. This would have been a rather unsavory working class area on the South Bank of the Thames. The title of the chapter, which began with a rain barrel, is finally explained.

Chapter VIII: The Baker Street Irregulars

Questions:

1. How have the murderers escaped?

2. Why do you think that the man with the wooden leg had been "'always knockin' about'" Mr. Smith's boatyard?

3. What information does Holmes get from Mrs. Smith's about the steam launch without appearing to question her?

4. Watson says that he thinks their course is plain. What objection do you think that Holmes will make to his proposal about what he and Holmes should do? What course do you think that Holmes will propose (since it is certain to be different)?

5. What does Watson's determination to see that Miss Morstan receives the portion of the treasure to which she is entitled indicate about his character? (Clue: Miss Morstan becoming an heiress fundamentally changes their relationship.)

6. The (fictitious) account in Holmes' almanac is full of unthinking, automatic racism quite typical of the Empire period. What further evidence of racism do you find either in its text or in Holmes' reaction to that text?

Commentary:

Holmes shows a great deal more tolerance of Toby than he often shows of humans: the difference is that Toby uses his natural abilities to the full, whereas Holmes cannot tolerate humans who fail to make full use of their intelligence.

The presentation of working class people in the novel is as problematic to a modern reader as is the representation of people of color. Doyle (and therefore Holmes) appears to assume that social distinctions are the result of evolutionary determinism, as though the poor in England (like the natives of the Andaman Islands) are lower on Darwin's evolutionary ladder than are the gentry class, to which, of course, Holmes and Watson belong. As a result, as Rosemary Jann points out, the behavior of the working classes is seen as predictable since it is "in some unspecified way innate or intrinsic ..., natural rather than cultural, the cause rather than the effect of their [inferiority] ... The quasi-biological determinism assumed in the stories reaffirms the status quo by providing a physical rationale for the lower classes' subordination to material conditions and provides an intangible basis for the higher classes' claims to transcend them" (70).

Sherlock Holmes learns that he has underestimated Jonathan Small who has laid his plans carefully, and it is refreshing to hear him admit that the criminals are "'sharper'" than he expected. For once, his reliance on stereotypes has let him down. Small did not simply chance on Mr. Smith's boatyard but had arranged his escape in advance with Smith. It is by no means clear, however, why the *Aurora* left with so little fuel when there is a large pile of coke on the wharf.

Holmes' contempt for the official police comes across in his assertions, "I have a fancy for working it out myself ..." Condescendingly, he tells Watson that he will bring in Inspector Jones at the last minute to protect his reputation. The newspaper report delights Holmes by its exaggerated praise of the abilities of Inspector Jones whom he considers to be a bungler at best. Knowing the care with which Jonathan Small has planned his crime, Holmes uses this to his advantage. Because the perpetrators will be confident that they have evaded pursuit, and since another man is under arrest for the murder, they have no reason to seek to leave the country but are likely to lay low in their hiding place.

Certain elements of the Holmes' stories have entered the popular imagination. Amongst these are the famous address 221B Baker Street, the foggy streets of London, and the Baker Street Irregulars, street-wise boys who know every part of London. The Irregulars are the stuff of romantic fiction: poor boys who are nevertheless respectful and disciplined. The way Holmes handles the boys is supposed to show his common touch, and the respect which they clearly have for him adds to the reader's admiration of his powers.

The account of the Andamanese which Holmes reads is quite accurate. They were rumored to be cannibals, though in the twentieth century this was questioned. Under four feet tall is hyperbole: somewhat below five feet would be more accurate. The reference to their "'hideous ... large, misshapen heads'" in the gazetteer is another piece of racial evolution theory. (If you search photograph of Andaman Islanders on the Internet, you will see that it is simply not true.) The one thing that Holmes' gazetteer leaves out, of course, is that the British invaded the Andaman Islands and made determined efforts to exterminate the natives who fiercely defended their land and culture.

Holmes' outstanding ability on the violin appears incongruous beside his skill in the boxing ring, but it adds to the mystique of this remarkable man.

Chapter IX: A Break in the Chain

Questions:

1. Why is Watson going to see Miss Morstan? Why does he at first claim that he is going to see Mrs. Cecil Forrester?

2. Holmes tells Watson that he has a good idea where the *Aurora* must be, so where could the boat be? (Actually, this is not such a difficult question as you might think. Where on a river could you put a boat so that it would not be immediately visible from either the river or the land?)

3. Explain the various ways in which Mr. Athelney Jones attempts to save face in his conversation with Dr. Watson.

4. At precisely what point did you as reader know that the old mariner was Sherlock Holmes? What was the clue to the man's true identity?

5. How does Mr. Athelney Jones attempt to save face after Holmes reveals his true identity?

Commentary:

In exclaiming, "'It is a romance!'" and describing the likeness of the story to unrealistic myths, Mrs. Forrester comes close to undercutting the credibility of the narrative. I think that this indicates that Doyle himself did not take his novel too seriously: he was writing to a sensationalist formula and he knew it. Miss Morstan proves herself to be the stereotypical innocent princess in a tower, incapable of helping herself and totally dependent upon men to save her - or in this case, to save her fortune.

Here is a timeline of the investigation so far:

- Day 1: July 8th - Miss Morstan's visit; murder of Bartholomew Sholto discovered.
- Day 2: July 9th - Holmes and Watson track the culprits; Holmes engages the help of the Baker Street Irregulars.
- Day 3: July 10th - An entire day without any sign of the fugitives or of the *Aurora*.
- Day 4: July 11th - Disguised as a seaman, Holmes goes looking for the *Aurora*.

Holmes is frustrated because he has reached the limit of what pure reasoning can achieve. Searching (what the official police would call "leg work") is much less interesting to Holmes. By the morning of Day 4, Holmes has been awake for around ninety-six hours. This is not physically impossible, but sleep deprivation on this scale would impact Holmes' physical and mental faculties. In other words, it works much better in fiction than it does in real life.

The Sign of Four by Sir Arthur Conan Doyle

Holmes flatters Watson's vanity when he tells him "'you can be much more useful if you will remain here as my representative.'" The fact is that Holmes needs to work inconspicuously (hence the disguise), and with Watson that would not be possible. The reader will recall that Watson himself suggested advertising for information about the missing boat, but that Holmes rejected the idea on the grounds that it would alert the murderers to the fact that they were suspects. At that time, Holmes felt it more useful to make them feel that they had safely got away and that an innocent man was likely to be tried for their crime. Now, however, Thaddeus Sholto has been exonerated (though it is far from clear on what grounds) and so the former objection is no longer valid. Also, to state the obvious, Holmes is running out of alternatives.

The official police being quite unable to solve the case has become an essential element of the private detective novel. Mr. Athelney Jones, having failed utterly to solve the crime himself, now actively seeks Holmes' assistance. The ubiquitous Mrs. Hudson does not appear to escort the old sailor into Mr. Holmes' rooms which is odd. Holmes is something of a practical joker, frequently exploiting Watson's rather gullible nature. In several of the stories, Holmes is able completely to deceive his friend by wearing a disguise, leaving Watson to speculate on the loss to the theater when Holmes decided to become a detective.

Since, by Holmes' own account, the owner of the boat repair yard where the *Aurora* is being hidden is rather suspicious (because there is nothing at all *wrong* with the boat's rudder), it is perhaps surprising that neither he nor any of the men working in his yard responded to the advertisement which Holmes placed in *The Standard*. Perhaps they simply did not have time to do so since Holmes himself discovered the boat only hours after the advertisement appeared.

Holmes once again insists that he have complete control of the operation to apprehend the two criminals, "'You are welcome to all the official credit, but you must act on the line that I point out. Is that agreed?'" He seeks no public acknowledgement for his part in their capture. Being a gentleman of independent means, the amateur detective seeks only the challenge of the 'game,' but Holmes' vanity requires that it is he who plays the game.

Quite how the Baker Street Irregulars failed to spot a steam launch either in dry dock or in a repair shed in a boatyard is hard to understand. Certainly, the *Aurora* would have been on private property and at least partially obscured, but for these lads neither *should* have been an insurmountable obstacle.

Holmes' action in ensuring that Watson gets to take the treasure to Miss Morstan is completely contrary to his expressed cynicism on the subject of women and matrimony. In fact, Holmes is setting his friend up in what he thinks will be the ideal situation for a proposal. That Inspector Jones would agree to such a proposal is not credible.

Chapter X: The End of the Islander

Questions:

1. Evaluate the reasoning by which Holmes concludes that Jonathan Small has not already left his hiding place, but that they are likely to do so on this particular evening. Watson says, "'It seems to me to be a little weak.'" Do you agree?

2. What do you think is the solution to the location of the getaway boat. How has it been hidden so effectively?

3. Suggest at least one method of locating the two fugitives that Holmes has, inexplicably, not employed.

4. There is something almost comically absurd about the method Holmes devises for his Street Arab to signal the approach of the men towards the launch. Can you say what it is? (Clue: Like most middle class people, Doyle knew very little about what really poor people kept in their pockets.)

5. How does Doyle make his description of the chase exciting?

6. What words and phrases are used to stress the Andaman Islander is more animal than human? Look for examples right up to the end of the chapter

Commentary:

Holmes certainly covers a wide range of, entirely unconnected, subjects which is a sure sign of his state of heightened intellectual excitement (and perhaps sleep-deprivation). Doyle takes advantage of a lull in the action to allow Holmes to explain the reasoning behind his location of the *Aurora*. It is important to the story to do this now as following Small's arrest the focus will be on his account of the Agra Treasure. Two explanations coming together would be undramatic.

Doyle's description of Mordecai Smith represents a stereotypical view of working people as feckless and drunken. It is quite remarkable that such a man has succeeded in running what appears to be a reasonably successful boat yard. (After all, he owns one of the fastest and newest boats on the river).

Holmes is certainly something of a 'control freak.' Everything must be done exactly as he has planned it, and he condescendingly rejects every idea that is not his own, saying, "'No, I thought over every possible course, and this is the best.'" Holmes' arrogance is obvious.

Watson is guilty of unthinking (and frankly repulsive) racism in his description of Small's companion, "Never have I seen features so deeply marked with all bestiality and cruelty ... his thick lips were writhed back from his teeth, which grinned and chattered at us with a half animal fury." He simply repeats the accepted view of his day that races have certain characteristics and can be arranged in an evolutionary hierarchy from the most savage to the most civilized. (That would be British, naturally!) Thus, he describes the Islander as only half human and half animal. When it comes to shooting the man, neither Holmes nor Watson hesitates for a moment. True, he is about to fire a poisoned dart at them, and they can therefore justify their action as self-defense. Note that Watson is terribly affected by how close he has come to death, "it turned me sick to think of the horrible death which had passed so close to us that night." He is, however, dismissive about the actual death of the Islander.

Chapter XI: The Great Agra Treasure

Questions:

1. What was Jonathan Small's original plan on the night of Bartholomew Sholto's murder? Why was he not able to carry out this plan?

2. Predict Miss Morstan's reaction when the treasure box is opened in her presence.

3. Explain Watson's reaction to the loss of the Agra treasure. Comment on his use of the metaphor, "'the golden barrier was gone from between us.'"

Commentary:

Jonathan Small says quite confidently, "'I don't believe that I can swing over the job,'" meaning that he cannot face a murder charge over the death of Bartholomew Sholto since he did not intend the man's death, was not the person who committed the murder, and was not even in the room when the murder was committed. In British Law, however, all of those involved in a crime in which a man is killed are held to be legally guilty of murder. The attitudes of Small and Holmes now that the 'game' is over are typical of those Holmes stories where the criminal is not actually evil. Neither bears the other ill-will. In fact, Holmes immediately offers to testify in Small's defense at the trial because he recognizes that the man is not by nature a murderer. Like other characters in the novel, Small's inherent English morality has been contaminated by his contact with India.

The classic detective story ends with an explanation of the solution to the crime by the detective who has normally gathered together all of the suspects. Doyle had not yet developed this formula, however, and in three of the novels (the exception being *The Hound of the Baskervilles*) the final part of the story is given over to the apprehended criminal who tells what the detective cannot know, the full background to the crime. This is where Doyle's love of the exotic, the adventurous, and the romantic is given full rein - a feature of the stories that Holmes can simply blame on Watson.

Why Jones should allow Watson to take the heavy, locked box to Miss Morstan is hard to explain except in terms of the author's determination to add romance to the heady mixture of his story. Watson describes the box thus, "A solid iron chest of Indian workmanship stood upon the deck. This, there could be no question, was the same that had contained the ill-omened treasure of the Sholtos. There was no key, but it was of considerable weight." Remember this description when you are reading Jonathan Small's account of the stealing and hiding of the treasure. The size and weight of the chest appears to vary quite considerably. For the moment, note that it is of "considerable weight" even though (as we later discover) it is empty. Imagine how much heavier it would have been with the jewels inside it. One wonders quite how a one-legged man and a very small native could have carried it six miles to Mr. Smith's boatyard. Incidentally, it is strange that, once they have possession of it, no one notices that the chest is empty. Even if the chest itself is heavy, the fact that there is nothing rattling around inside it would indicate that there is nothing inside.

It is very convenient for Watson (though unlikely given the state of the investigation) that Mrs. Forrester should choose to leave Mary Morstan alone for the evening. Notice how surprisingly unenthusiastic Mary Morstan is about the treasure; she knows as well as Watson that inheriting such a vast sum would make it impossible for him to propose to her. The scene where Watson declares his love for Miss Morstan and is accepted by her is pure sentimental romance. Watson behaves like a perfect gentleman and Miss Morstan like a perfect lady.

Chapter XII: The Strange Story of Jonathan Small

Questions:

1. By what arguments does Abdullah Khan succeed in persuading Small to join the conspiracy to rob and murder Achmet?
2. Make sure that you add the events described by Small to your timeline.
3. In what ways is the ending of the novel merely conventional (i.e., an ending which rewards the virtuous and punishes the guilty, which reasserts order over chaos, and which leaves the reader reassured that (much as they have enjoyed this peek into an exotic, adventurous, criminal underworld) they will be able to sleep safe in their beds tonight?

Commentary:

The villainy in many of the Holmes short stories and three out of four of the novels has its origin in foreign parts, lands where extreme violence and extreme passions are more the norm than in Victoria's England. As Rosemary Jann points out, readers "usually prefer the striking and the bizarre to the merely criminal" (75).

Small explains tipping the treasure into the Thames "'rather than let it go to kith or kin of Sholto or of Morstan.'" That he should wish to keep it out of the hands of Sholto's descendents is reasonable given that Sholto stole the treasure from The Four, although it directly contradicts the statement he has just given that he had "'no quarrel whatever'" with young Bartholomew Sholto and no wish to kill him. However, Captain Morstan appears to have behaved honorably to Small throughout, so what objection could be have to his daughter inheriting a portion of the treasure? Small's claim to have always acted in the interests of the other three who made the initial agreement as much as in his own interest further establishes his honorable motives, but it is hardly convincing since, as he himself admits, they are still locked up on Andaman and there is nothing he could do about that.

Jonathan Small's story of joining the Army must have been a common one. Although there was great pride in the feats of British Arms around the globe, individual soldiers were recruited from the poorest class and were regarded as 'the scum of the earth.' Small's injury is as mobile as that of Dr. Watson. Originally, the crocodile takes off his leg "'just above the knee,'" but then he has "'enough knee left to keep good grip on the saddle.'" This is simply inconsistent.

Small's account of the Indian Mutiny is colored by the prejudices of his race. The natives are "'black fiends [...] dancing and howling round the burning house'" whilst the plucky British are bravely defending themselves and their families though massively outnumbered in "'a fight of the millions against the hundreds.'" The action of the natives is presented as particularly perfidious since they have been trained and armed by the very British who they are slaughtering. In truth, there were (as usual in war) atrocities on both sides of the conflict.

Jonathan Small refers to "'the innumerable gates'" on the western walls of Agra Fort. Surely that would rather defeat the whole idea of the fortification. A map of Agra fort on the Internet shows only two main gates (one to the south and one to the west). Small really does not have much alternative to joining the conspiracy. Notice that he only does so having ensured that the safety of the fort will not be compromised. In such ways, Doyle establishes that he is basically an honorable (British) man. The rajah remains a vague and unconvincing character and his cunning plan to divide his wealth as a way of preserving it hardly bears scrutiny.

Notice how Jonathan Small defends his actions by appealing to the different situation in which he find himself: life seems more valuable in Victorian England than it did in the middle of the Indian Mutiny. Rosemary Jann points out that, "Foreigners are always treated as exotics by Doyle, as if to imply that the infection of British normalcy is more plausible when it comes from exposure to alien contagions" (76). Even the treachery of Major Sholto is placed in the context of his years of arduous service in India and the temptation placed in his way by the plan of The Four to retrieve the hidden treasure. Sensing that his listeners are judging him harshly, Small reminds them that his choice was between having his own throat cut and joining in the crime that would make him rich for life. He not unreasonably asks how many men would have acted as he did.

The idea that the three men left the treasure out in the open while Mohamet Singh guarded the gate and the other three carried Achmet's body "'some distance off'" for a hurried burial seems preposterous. Surely one of them would have guarded it since anyone could have come along and found it? Similarly, the robbers appear to have opened the box in the street and then made an inventory (presumably in writing) of each of the hundreds of items. Once again, anyone could have come along (even though it was night in a seldom visited part of the fort). On a more mundane point, where did they get the pencil and paper? Small reports, "A thorough search was quickly made, and the body was discovered." The search cannot, however, have been particularly thorough since it failed to uncover the treasure which was hidden in the same hall.

Given that gemstones tend to be small, the box described recovered by Holmes might have been large enough to contain everything that Small lists, though one presumes that sufficient packing was used to present the stones from rolling around inside. There is no way, however, that such a haul could have been contained in the "bundle" in the merchant's hand.

Small will explain that he was sent to prison on the Andaman Islands where he was one of the very few white prisoners. This would certainly have been true since the Andamans were used only for native political prisoners. How Small and his native accomplices got sent there is never explained. Klinger reports that the population of Andaman natives fell from 3,000-3,500 in the 1850s to around 400 by 1895. The British not only tried to exterminate the natives with military attacks, but they unwittingly introduced diseases against which the islanders had no natural immunity (Klinger ed. 366).

Notice the coded language in which Small speaks to Sholto. Small stands up for his three co-conspirators treating them as in every way his equal and rejecting the racism of Major Sholto:

"'What have three black fellows to do with our agreement?'

"'Black or blue,' said I, 'they are in with me, and we all go together.'"

This is another way in which Small's honorable nature is evident. However, he shows great naiveté in trusting Major Sholto to find the treasure and then to carry out his obligations not only to The Four but also to Morstan, particularly since doing so will cut Sholto's share of the treasure by four fifths. Perhaps Small, who was a regular soldier, simply has an inflated idea of the honor of the officers and gentlemen with whom he is dealing.

Small recounts being told by Morstan that Sholto went off to India because, "His uncle had died, leaving him a fortune." This was clearly a cover story to explain Sholto's sudden wealth the true source of which was the treasure. Small certainly believed it to be so, though perhaps Morstan might have found it harder to believe that a fellow officer would be so treacherous. The fact that Morstan was not involved in Sholto's treachery and behaved honorably to The Four throughout makes Small's earlier statement that he dumped the treasure in the Thames to prevent it falling into the hands of descendents of either Sholto or Morstan inexplicable.

Given the hostility of the Islanders (which has been stated in no uncertain terms) it seems hard to believe that "a little Andaman Islander was picked up by a convict-gang in the woods." Why would they be concerned about him, particularly since he was pretty much at death's door? It seems more likely that finding an enemy at such a disadvantage they would simply have killed him.

Presumably when Small says, "I made friends with someone who could help me," he is referring to some member of Major Sholto's household since everything in his plans, including getting access to the room of Bartholomew Sholto, suggests that he had inside help. The obvious candidate is the housekeeper. Who better than she would know Bartholomew Sholto's supper time? Holmes, however, with no supporting evidence will identify the confederate as Lal Rao, the butler. In saying that it "'could be no other,'" he is influenced by the race of the occupants of the house.

Small appears to retain faith with his three co-conspirators. He speaks as though he had every intention, once he reclaimed the treasure, of seeking out the others and making sure they got their share however unrealistic such a plan actually is. It is also surprising that he did not make straight for London given his burning desire for revenge against Sholto. The ever-honorable Small takes care to establish that Mr. Smith had no knowledge of the murder of Bartholomew or of the theft of the treasure. Small is aware that Smith is a family man and that if he were to go to jail his family would be destitute.

Rather uncharacteristically, Holmes admits that there is one thing he had not thought of: it had not occurred to him that Tonga having dropped all of his other darts would still have one dart in his blow-pipe. Actually, it seems a little unlikely that Tonga would have kept his darts during all the years of his travels with Small, or that, if he had done so, the poison on the darts would still have been lethal. Finally, 'loading' a dart into a blow-pipe is not quite the same as loading a gun; whereas a bullet is securely held in its chamber, a dart is likely to fall out of a blow-pipe.

Doyle finally gets around to explaining that Small and Tonga brought with them the rope that Small used to get into the window of Bartholomew Sholto's room. He leaves it until now in the assurance that the reader will have forgotten the details. The idea that, even with a rope, a one-legged man would find it relatively easy to climb sixty feet up the outside of a building is frankly unrealistic; the idea of such a diminutive figure as Tonga winding a very long rope around himself and then climbing up the sides of the house is incredible, as is the detail that "'Tonga then pulled up the rope, closed the window, and made off the way that he had come.'" It would actually have been much easier to throw the end of the rope down to Small, and the absence of the rope would have made it hard for even Holmes to work out how Small got into the high room. Then there is the large hook in the wall of Bartholomew's room (remember the hook?). Since Small does not mention that they brought that with them, it was a tremendous stroke of luck to find it there!

The dating of Watson's marriage in the stories is, frankly, inconsistent. Much ink has been expended in trying to explain the inconsistencies, but it is much more likely that Doyle simply did not keep a note on his own chronology. Watson does marry in one of the later stories, so presumably Mary dies. However, when Holmes refers to that later marriage, he makes no reference to Watson having been married before. Holmes' reaction to the proposed marriage appears to be unfeeling to say the least, but it is perfectly clear that it is an act mostly designed to make fun of poor Watson - in which Holmes succeeds. Consider, however, that by the marriage Holmes knows that he will be losing a close and utterly reliable friend, an invaluable assistant in his investigations, and a devoted (if overly romantic) chronicler. The marriage is another indication that, at this stage, Doyle had no intention of writing more novels featuring Sherlock Holmes and that the idea of short stories had not yet occurred to him.

At least in his early years as the world's only consulting detective, Holmes is not a rich man despite having an independent income. (One suspects that elder brother Mycroft would make sure he does not starve). This is clear because he needed someone to share the rent of the very modest rooms in Baker Street. From this case, he makes not a penny, since there is no reward either for the recovery of the treasure (which has actually been lost) or for the arrest of the murderer. Later in his career, he will tell clients that he has a strict scale of charges and occasionally a very rich client will reward him handsomely. However, for Holmes wealth is as unimportant as public acknowledgement; for Holmes the game's the thing.

Studying the Novel

People often ask me whether I knew the end of a Sherlock Holmes story before I started it. Of course I do. One could not possibly steer a course if one did not know one's destination. The first thing is to get your idea. Having got that key idea one's next task is to conceal it and lay emphasis upon everything which can make for a different explanation. Holmes, however, can see all the fallacies of the alternatives, and arrives more or less dramatically to the true solution by steps which he can describe and justify. (*Sir Arthur Conan Doyle*, Bloom ed. 75-6).

Amongst the four Holmes novels, *The Sign of Four* is judged by most critics to be inferior to *The Hound of the Baskervilles*, but much better than either *A Study in Scarlet* or *The Valley of Fear*. Neilson sums up the strengths and weaknesses of the novel:

The Sign of Four is praised for its picture of Holmes in action and the ingenuity of the initial puzzle, for its evocation of the atmosphere of London in the 1880's, for its sharp delineation of character, and for its dramatic effectiveness. It is sometimes faulted, however, for a plot too closely reminiscent of Wilkie Collins's *The Moonstone* (1868), a solution that comes too early in the narrative, and for Jonathan Small's overly long confession.

Chronology of the Case

[Note: Dates marked c. (circa) are conjectural - a 'best guess' based on the text.]

1857 - At the Siege of Agra, Jonathan Small and three native accomplices murder the secret courier of a rich Indian raj and steal an immensely valuable treasure in jewels which they hide in the walls of part of the fort. The Four are arrested for murder and sent to prison on the Andaman Islands.

c. 1861 - Mary Morstan is born in India. Her mother dies either during, or as a consequence of, child-birth.

c. 1865 - Mary Morstan is placed in a respectable boarding school in Edinburgh.

c. 1876 - The Four make an agreement with Major John Sholto and Captain Morstan to retrieve the treasure and to share it five ways (Sholto and Morstan each getting equal shares of one fifth of the treasure).

Sholto leaves the Andamans for India with a treasure map. Having apparently inherited a considerable fortune, Major Sholto resigns his commission, returns to England, and retires to Upper Norwood where he purchases Pondicherry Lodge.

1878 - Captain Morstan is granted one year's leave from the Army of India and returns to England.

December 2nd - Captain Morstan visits Major Sholto - they argue over the treasure and Morstan dies of a heart attack.

December 3rd - Mary Morstan goes to the Langham Hotel in London to meet her father as arranged, but he has disappeared.

c. 1880 - With the help of the native Tonga, Jonathan Small escapes from the prison on the Andaman Islands.

1882

January or February - Major Sholto receives a letter from India the contents of which shock him badly.

April 28th - Major John Sholto confesses everything to his twin sons (Bartholomew and Thaddeus). He sees Jonathan Small looking into his window, and dies before he can reveal where the treasure is hidden.

End of April or the beginning of May - The Sholto brothers start digging for the treasure. Holmes says, "'they were six years looking for it.'"

May 4th - An advertisement appears in the *London Times* seeking the address of Miss Mary Morstan to which she replies.

c. May 7th - A box containing a single pearl arrives for Miss Morstan. In each of the next five years (1883-8), another pearl is sent on the same date. The pearls come from a chaplet, the single piece of the treasure which the Major took out before hiding everything else.

1888

July 6th - Bartholomew Sholto finally discovers the treasure in the garret. Informed of this by an employee in the house, Small and Tonga enter Bartholomew's room on the top storey of Pondicherry Lodge. In the process, Bartholomew is killed by Tonga.

July 7th - Thaddeus Sholto posts a letter to Mary Morstan telling her to be at the Lyceum Theater at 7 p.m. that evening with two friends. He says that the treasure was discovered "'only yesterday,'" that is July 6th.

Picking Faults

> [A]ccuracy of detail matters little. I have never striven for it and have made some bad mistakes in consequence. What matter if I hold my readers? (Conan Doyle quoted in Booth 157)

Paradoxically, detective fiction, surely one of the most popular of genres, and Sir Arthur Conan Doyle, unarguably its most popular exponent, have received relatively little attention or respect from literary critics. Indeed, in a famous essay written in 1975, "Literature High and Low: The Case of the Mystery Story," critic Geoffrey Hartman argued that the detective genre is, by its very nature, incapable of producing great literature:

> Most popular mysteries are devoted to solving rather than examining a problem. Their reasonings put reason to sleep, abolish darkness by elucidation, and bury the corpse for good. Few detective novels want the reader to exert his intelligence fully, to

find gaps in the plot or the reasoning, to worry about the moral question of fixing the blame. They are exorcisms, stories with happy endings that could be classified with comedy because they settle the unsettling. As to the killer, he is often a bogeyman chosen by the "finger" of the writer after it has wavered suspensefully between this and that person for the right number of pages ... The *surnaturel* is *explique*, and the djinni returned to the bottle by a trick. For the mystery story has always been a genre in which appalling facts are made to fit into a rational or realistic pattern. (Quoted by Clausson)

It is not necessary to agree with Hartman's sweeping condemnation of an entire genre to find that much of his criticism is entirely valid in relation to this particular novel.

The writing in *The Sign of Four* shows signs of being hurried and, frankly slip-shod. Farrell concedes it faults when he writes, "That the novel is formulaic and often meretricious [attention-grabbing in a rather crude way] may be undeniable" (48). The book should not be mistaken for 'great literature' despite its continuing popularity and its justified claim to be a classic of the detective genre. Emphasizing their contemporary context, Pearsall states that the first two novels of the Holmes' saga "were routine productions of no great consequence. The class of reader who bought such books would be looking for an easy read." Indeed, Doyle himself regarded his popular fiction as 'potboilers,' markedly inferior to the historical novels on which he felt that his reputation would rest. At the time he was writing this second Holmes novel, Doyle was also at work on *The White Company* an historical novel for which he did extensive research and which he regarded as a higher form of writing.

In a 2014 essay, "Poe's 'The Murders in the Rue Morgue' and Doyle's *The Sign of Four*," Bertman sets out in detail the parallels between these two works and argues that "Doyle, without ever acknowledging his source, took his novel's basic plot from Poe's short story." He further notes that "In 1901 Simon Sidney Teiser, then an undergraduate at the University of Virginia, charged [Doyle] with piracy in a published essay provocatively titled 'Is Doyle a Plagiarist?'" It is not necessary, however, to go outside the novel itself to find weaknesses. There are a number of improbabilities, inconsistencies, and outright contradictions in the narrative. The following sections bring together the major points already covered in the commentary.

1. Watson and Holmes as authors

Since Holmes and Watson began sharing the Baker Street rooms in 1884, they have been living together approximately four years and four months as *The Sign of Four* opens. It is true that Watson did not publish *A Study in Scarlet* until 1887, but why he has waited a year to mention to Holmes his having written "'a small brochure with the somewhat fantastic title of "A Study in Scarlet"'" is inexplicable. Even more difficult to understand is the need for Holmes to draw Watson's attention to his own publications, which have been on the shelves in the same sitting room that he has shared with Watson. The room is really not that big! Of course, the answer is that Doyle has to find a way of informing *the reader* of these things, but that is no excuse for clumsy writing.

Between *A Study in Scarlet* and *The Sign of Four*, Watson would eventually record fourteen other cases, but Doyle had no thought of writing these when he published the second Holmes novel. The void between the two novels explains why Doyle feels the need to have Holmes improbably remind his friend that he is the world's only consulting detective, and to give him two demonstrations of his methods. It also explains why Watson gives the impression that he is not used to participating in his friend's investigations. In the light of the later short stories, none of this makes sense.

2. The date on which the case begins and of the crime

Writing to J. M. Stoddart, editor of *Lippincott's Magazine* which first published the novel in serial form, Doyle pointed to a glaring error, "By the way there is one very obvious mistake which must be corrected in book form - in the second chapter the letter is headed July 7th, and on almost the same page I talk of its being a September evening." Strangely, the mistake never has been corrected (Klinger ed. 234).

A glance at the chronology of the case reveals obvious problems. The Agra treasure remains hidden for twenty years before it is retrieved by Major Sholto. Given that the Four concealed the heavy chest in the wall rather quickly (they were arrested for murder on the following day) and that the room was searched for the dead merchant's body, Major Sholto was rather fortunate to find it still in situ. It is five more years before Jonathan Small's appearance at Sholto's window, since upon his escape he and Tonga did not go straight to London to locate Sholto. A further six years elapses between the Sholto brothers learning of the hidden treasure from their dying father and Bartholomew locating it in the attic. This seems to be an improbably long time (the house and grounds at Pondicherry Lodge cannot be so very vast) during which Jonathan Small and Tonga apparently make a living exhibiting Tonga at fairs without becoming celebrities in an age that loved sensations (think of General Tom Thumb [1838 - 1883] and Joseph Carey Merrick, the Elephant Man [1862 - 1890]). Thirty-one years elapse between Jonathan Small having the treasure in his hands (briefly) in the fort of Agra and his repossessing it at Pondicherry Lodge. Put simply, various elements of the plot simply do not hang together.

3. Weaknesses in Holmes' Reasoning

Clausen points out that though Holmes claims to use only observation, logic and knowledge in his detection, the reality is much less pure:

> Whether Holmes' methods and results in his detecting career really satisfy scientific standards of rigor is another question entirely. It has often been pointed out that many of his deductions are far from airtight. Although he frequently denounces guesswork, at times he seems alarmingly dependent on lucky intuitions ... The important point, however, is that he is conceived - and conceives of himself - as a man who applies scientific methods to the detection of crime, and that his success as a detective is due to those methods. He uses them more convincingly than most other fictional detectives, and he hews to them with a religious intensity. (Bloom ed. 84)

Although Holmes is frequently seen performing chemistry experiments, these very seldom have any direct application to his investigations. There are also a number of examples where Holmes' methods are far less impressive than they seem at first glance. Here we shall examine the two demonstrations that Doyle contrives before the start of the case, the point of which is to establish, or remind us, what scientific detection is.

a) Watson's telegram

Holmes observes "'a little reddish mould [soil] adhering'" to the instep of Watson's shoe which he identifies as unique to Seymour Street in which he knows that the pavement has been dug up. From this, he concludes that Watson has visited the post office in that street, and since he knows Watson has not written a letter that morning, and that he has an ample supply of stamps, he deduces that his friend must have gone there to send a telegram: the amazed, and baffled, Watson confirms the truth of this conclusion.

Passing rapidly over the unlikely detail of Seymour Street uniquely having "'earth of this peculiar reddish tint,'" and the fact that Watson might simply have been walking *past* the post office on Seymour Street (which was no great distance from Baker Street) to go somewhere else, Holmes ignores other reasons why Watson might have gone to the Post Office. Perhaps he went to collect a parcel, or to buy a postal order, or to make an enquiry. Doyle typically discourages the reader from seeing the holes in the reasoning by ensuring that Holmes is right.

b) Watson's watch

Holmes is able correctly to identify the owner of the pocket watch and to describe the man's character despite the fact that he has no prior knowledge that Watson even had an elder brother. Some of his reasoning, for example from the initials engraved on the watch, is water-tight, but some is not. Holmes observes "'thousands of scratches all around the hole-marks where the key has slipped,'" and from this he concludes that Watson's brother was habitually drunk since "'you will never see a drunkard's watch without [such scratches].'" There are, however, plenty of other explanations for the scratches. Perhaps the brother suffered from a disease which made his hand unsteady, such as Parkinson's; perhaps he was in the habit of winding his watch in the dark; or perhaps he was simply as careless in winding his watch as he was in his general use of the watch whose case is dented and scratched.

4. The route from the Lyceum Theater to Brixton

Martin Booth points out that, being relatively new to London when he wrote the early Holmes stories, Doyle's knowledge of the city was somewhat limited:

[He] drew most of his early information from street maps, never visiting the places where he set the action. The result is that a site in London is often actually given the description of streets he had known in the Edinburgh of his student days, the Birmingham he had visited when working for Dr. Hoare, and the less salubrious areas of Portsmouth. (Booth 157)

In *The New Annotated Sherlock Holmes*, Volume 3, Leslie Klinger traces Watson's description of the route taken by the carriage in great detail (see pages 243-5). The bottom line is that a few of the roads named in the text no longer existed by 1888, some were not roads at all but buildings, and not all of the roads actually meet each other, so it would have been literally impossible to have followed this exact route. To this, Doyle would doubtless reply that what matters is the *impression* of the journey not its strict geographical accuracy.

5. The account of the crime

Having been informed by a source inside the Sholto household of the discovery of the treasure, Jonathan Small's initial plan is to enter Bartholomew Sholto's room at a time when he will be at supper and to search for the Agra treasure. Unfortunately, when Tonga gains access through the roof, he finds Bartholomew sitting in his chair and impulsively shoots a poisoned dart from his blowpipe. After Small has gained entry through the window, a search of the room reveals the treasure with which they make off. Their escape down-river has been previously arranged with the boatman, Mr. Mordecai Smith.

This scenario, however, contains many improbabilities:

- Tonga has to climb up the outside of the building, in the dark, carrying a blowpipe and a sixty-foot rope;
- Holmes concludes that the rope was secured in this way, "one end of it [was tied] to this great hook in the wall." However, it is never definitively explained whether the hook was already in the room (and if so why) or whether it was yet another thing that Tonga carried;

- For an untrained man with a wooden leg, climbing up the outside of a building using rope would be a daunting challenge;
- There are at least three servants in the house, none of whom apparently hears or sees anything.

6. The investigation of the crime

From his examination of the crime scene, Holmes is able to deduce how the 'locked room' was entered, to put a name to the man who entered by the window, and to give a description of the man who entered by the roof. All of this is achieved by observation of the clues left behind (notably foot marks and the poisoned dart) and by linking these to what he has already heard from Mary Morstan and Thaddeus Sholto about their fathers' histories.

There are, however, errors and weaknesses in Doyle's presentation of Holmes' investigation:

- Holmes finds lots of small footprints on the floor of the garret, but the garret has no floor as such; there are only joists which support a thin plaster ceiling. Had even the diminutive Tonga put his foot between the joists, it would have gone straight through;
- There is no way that Holmes can deduce the location of the intruders once they have made their get-away. By the time Holmes investigates the crime scene, they have been in their hideout for at least twenty hours. To resolve this, Doyle invents the broken carboy and the leaking creosote. How and when the carboy was cracked, and what Bartholomew wanted creosote for in the first place is never explained.
- Given the very distinctive appearance of the two intruders, it never occurs to Holmes to circulate their description.

7. The Story of the Agra Treasure

The story of the Agra Treasure adds the excitement of murder and betrayal in an exotic location. Doyle knew his audience.

The narrative of Jonathan Small, however, strains belief in several ways:

- It is unclear how, having had his leg bitten off above the knee, Small could have enough knee left to ride a horse;
- Why the three Indians should not just kill Small rather than make him an equal member of their conspiracy (thus cutting their share of the loot) is unclear;
- Why the Four were sent to the Andaman Islands, which was exclusively for political prisoners, is unexplained;
- The size and weight of the bundle or chest containing the treasure appears to change depending on circumstances;

- The probability of the chest remaining concealed in the wall from the night it was, rather quickly, hidden to the time, twenty years later, when Sholto found it is small;
- The description of how Tonga is supposed to have become dedicated to Small and how this facilitated their escape from the Andamans is unconvincing;
- Why Small did not return to England immediately and how he located Sholto are unexplained.

8. Trapping the Criminals

Holmes is completely responsible for finding Small and Tonga and for capturing them. This aspect of the plot is, however, also open to several objections:

- That the Baker Street Irregulars failed to spot the Aurora is strange;
- That one of the Irregulars should be carrying a white handkerchief with which to signal is unlikely;
- Holmes has no reason for being so confident that Small will try to escape on that particular night.

9. Characterization

Properly speaking there is only *one* character in the entire novel: Sherlock Holmes. All of the others, including Watson, are merely stereotypes - what E. M. Forster called 'flat characters' (*Aspects of the Novel*). Doyle's depiction of character relies on crude stereotyping. Of course, this is most evident in the portrayal of Tonga, of uneducated criminals, and of the laboring class in general, but it is also true of the police and of the refined ladies in the novel. Each is merely a representative of a type whose actions and reactions are entirely determined by their social position. Indeed, as the commentary has shown, much of Holmes deductive method depends on his confidence that individuals act and react in a way predetermined by their place in society.

Wilson writes in defense of Doyle, stressing the primacy of plot:

> The writing, of course, is full of clichés, but these clichés are dealt out with a ring which gives them a kind of value, while the author makes speed and saves space so effectively that we are rarely in danger of getting bogged down in anything boring. And the clichés of situation and character are somehow made to function, too, for the success of the general effect. (Bloom ed. 78)

In my commentary, however, I have repeatedly pointed out the use of negative stereotypes in the descriptions of poor and working class people and of Indian and Far Eastern natives. Doyle is unthinkingly repeating the prejudices of his time and of his class, and this must be seen as an artistic weakness.

Structure of a Sherlock Holmes Mystery

In his Introduction to *Classical Mystery Writers*, Bloom references the code which Borges used to defined the ideal tale of mystery and detection as comprising:

- A discretional maximum of six characters.
- Resolution of all loose ends to the mystery.
- Avaricious economy of means.
- Priority of how over who.
- Necessity and wonder of the solution.

He adds, "Whether or not the code is universal, Chesterton [in the Father Brown stories] observes it with classical rigor, and Conan Doyle does not" (Bloom ed. xi). In Doyle's defense, he was in the process of inventing the detective mystery as Borges knew it.

The typical Sherlock Holmes short story tends to follow this structure:

- Setting the scene in the Baker Street rooms;
- Enter a client;
- Watson can't deduce anything about the client, but Holmes can:
- The statement of the mystery by the client;
- Holmes questions the client;
- Holmes thinks through the problem;
- The investigation takes Holmes and Watson to the scene of the crime;
- Watson can't deduce anything from the crime-scene, but Holmes can;
- An obvious solution often exists, normally one put forward by the police, which points to an entirely innocent person;
- Holmes' observations and questioning prove this solution to be fallacious;
- Setting the trap and catching the criminal(s);
- The perpetrator(s) tells his/her story;
- Holmes explains how he solved the mystery.

In the case of the novels, the greatest deviation from this template is the inclusion of an extended narrative (almost a separate story) which gives the historical background to the mystery. In *A Study in Scarlet*, the back-story of Jefferson Hope's desire for revenge against Drebber, "The Country of the Saints," is told by an unidentified third person omniscient narrator who claims to be using Dr. Watson's Journal. It takes up almost half of the novel. The result is a structurally weakened story - to say nothing of the mystery of who is supposed to have written it down since it is not at all like Watson's first person narrative.

In *The Sign of Four*, the background narrative, though still extensive, is much shorter and is more convincingly integrated into the structure of the narrative being told in a single chapter by Jonathan Small immediately after his arrest. The problem of the historical background is solved even more effectively in *The Hound of the Baskervilles* where in Chapter Two, before the case has actually started, Dr. Mortimer reads a Baskerville family paper dating from 1742 which presents the legend of the hound. Since the perpetrator is killed at the climax to the story, this leaves Holmes to give a full account of the case to Watson in the final chapter. In the final Holmes' novel, *The Valley of Fear*, Doyle returns to the earlier structure with the narrative giving the background to the crime, entitled "The Scowrers," occupying Part II of the novel following Holmes' explanation of the solution of the crime.

"The Country of the Saints," "The Strange Story of Jonathan Small," and "The Scowrers" are essential because, since the crimes in three of the novels had their origins in America, India, and America respectively, there is much that detection simply cannot uncover. However, it is hard to escape the thought that in three of the novels at least, Doyle enjoyed writing the historical fiction rather more than he enjoyed writing the part involving Holmes.

Structure of The Sign of Four

Knight argues that Doyle's second Holmes novel marked a significant advance upon his first:

> It is structurally more successful than *A Study in Scarlet* - the historical material is, with [Wilkie] Collins's guidance, integrated better and there is much more action and mystery, though neither novella makes much of a puzzle of the culprits - Doyle is still working primarily in an adventure mode and the crime-revealing denouement ... is not yet part of his armoury. (Knight 58)

The Sign of Four begins with a "recapitulation touch [which] is necessary because it has been three years since the public has seen the pair" (Cox 43). This is followed by the interview with the client Mary Morstan. As the mystery develops, it becomes clear that there are a number of distinct but connected puzzles:

- How did Captain Morstan disappear?
- Who enquires about Miss Morstan's address and then sends her annually six pearls, and why?
- Who are the Four?
- How did Major Sholto come by the Indian treasure that he has hidden?
- Who is Jonathan Small and what is his connection to the treasure?

- Who killed Bartholomew Sholto, why and how?
- Where is the *Aurora* and the two men who hired the stream launch?

Some of these mysteries provide very little for even a man of Holmes' skills to work on. The solution to the first and second is basically provided by Thaddeus Sholto's narrative. Holmes' methods certainly illuminate the *who* and the *how* of Bartholomew Sholto's death, but the full explanation of motivation is only provided by Jonathan Small's narrative. Though a certain amount of deduction indicates where to look, Holmes finds the *Aurora* by using disguise and old-fashioned leg work.

To summarize, *The Sign of Four* is at least as much a tale of exotic adventure (with elements taken from the gothic novel) as it is a detective story. Whilst the solution to the mystery is to Holmes "an end in itself," so that he does not involve himself emotionally in the characters (Jann 22) Doyle appears less interested in the detection element in the story (which is effectively completed by the end of Chapter 7) than he is in weaving a grotesque and exciting plot with a dramatic chase at its climax.

In one particular aspect, this novel marks a great improvement upon *A Study in Scarlet* about which reviewers complained, quite accurately, that the reader is not given all of the information necessary to solve the crime and to identify the murderer. Holmes amazes everyone by arresting the cabman, but he is only able to do so because the name of the man has been forwarded to him by the Cleveland police. No such objection can be made to *The Sign of Four*, where the reader learns everything that Holmes learns. Cox concludes that the novel shows that Doyle "had his formula fully under control" (48) which is something of an exaggeration.

The Scientific Detective

> The project of the Sherlock Holmes stories is to dispel magic and mystery, to make everything explicit, accountable, subject to scientific analysis ... The stories are a plea for science not only in the spheres conventionally associated with detection (footprints, traces of hair or cloth, cigarette ends), where they have been deservedly influential on forensic practice, but in all areas. They reflect the widespread optimism characteristic of the period concerning the comprehensive power of positivist science. (Belsey in Hodgson ed. 383)

Knight is highly critical of Doyle's claim that his sleuth makes detection a science:

> Inside the scientific mumbo-jumbo , the learned baggage, the mystique of all-night pipe-smoking and austerely distant behaviour is someone who can apply the common knowledge of the human

tribe ... The essential power of Sherlock Holmes is that his substantial disciplinary authority is in fact enacted in a publicly accessible way: the ultimate methods of solving a crime are usually as simple as any used by the mid-century detective foot soldiers. (57)

This is undoubtedly true if the word 'scientific' is taken in its strictest sense for the obvious reason that forensic science was in its infancy in the final decade of the nineteenth century. Holmes does conduct a scientific experiment during the course of his investigation but it has no relevance to the problem in hand other than to take his mind off it. If, however, we take the word 'scientific' to apply to a method (a rational and logical approach to problem-solving) then it is fully justified.

In the image that most readers have of Sherlock Holmes, the great detective is associated with three iconic artifacts: the deerstalker hat, the pendulous Calabash Pipe, and the magnifying glass. Of these three, only the third is ever mentioned in the canon. The original illustrator, Sidney Paget, began showing Holmes wearing a deerstalker presumably because (as photographs attest) he frequently wore one himself. Although Holmes is frequently described as smoking a pipe (as well as cigarettes and cigars), the curved Calabash pipe is in neither the text nor Paget's early illustrations; it was an innovation by the actor William Gillette who first played the great detective on stage in 1900. (The actor found it impossible to deliver his lines with a straight pipe in his mouth, something which became possible when he switched to the curved, pendulous Calabash.) The magnifying glass, however, is omnipresent in the stories pointing us to the basis of Holmes' scientific methods.

Whilst Holmes is very fond of surprising both Watson and his clients with his powers of observation, it is in his detailed examination of the scene of the crime that these are shown to their best advantage. At the start of the novel when Holmes is describing to Watson his monograph differentiating one hundred and forty kinds of tobacco ash, Watson comments:

"You have an extraordinary genius for minutiae," I remarked.

"I appreciate their importance. Here is my monograph upon the tracing of footsteps ..."

Deduction depends upon data, and what differentiates Holmes from Watson, and from the official police, is that he painstakingly examines *everything*, whilst others examine *only what they prejudge to be significant*; where others look at the crime-scene through a filter of assumptions, Holmes collects all of the data before he begins to theorize. As Rosemary Jann points out:

Holmes' genius is largely a question of his ability to identify and interpret correctly those details that actually constitute the narrative of the crime ... He is able to determine which clues are relevant and to assemble them so as to reveal the solution, precisely because he does not expect facts to speak for themselves and is constantly testing them against hypotheses that his combination of observation, knowledge, and logic has already allowed him to form. (27 & 48).

Thus, in the present story, Watson describes Holmes' action as they ascend the stairs to Bartholomew Sholto's room:

> Twice as we ascended Holmes whipped his lens out of his pocket and carefully examined marks which appeared to me to be mere shapeless smudges of dust upon the cocoa-nut matting which served as a stair-carpet. He walked slowly from step to step, holding the lamp, and shooting keen glances to right and left.

Of course, the marks are not "shapeless smudges of dust," but they also turn out to have nothing at all to do with the murder. By his careful examination, however, Holmes has eliminated the stairs as the means by which a possible intruder from the outside could have gained access to Bartholomew Sholto's room.

Having observed, Holmes is able to infer from his raw data much more than can be seen, even with the aid of a magnifying glass, by the naked eye. To do this, Holmes uses reasoning to make inferences from his observations (i.e. to formulate an hypothesis based on the simplest and most likely explanation suggested by the relevant data). Such inferences are inevitably speculative, although Holmes frequently claims for them a reliability greater than that which logic alone would grant them (and Doyle manipulates the plot to ensure that Holmes is generally correct). One reason Holmes does this is simple vanity, but it is only fair to add that his inferences are supported by a vast wealth of relevant information which ranges from his encyclopedic knowledge of the chemistry of substances to his compendious knowledge of the history of crime.

Forming an hypothesis of the crime effectively means constructing a narrative (sometimes a number of competing narratives) that will cover the facts of the case as Holmes has identified them. In order to do this, Holmes has to do some silent thinking. When this point comes in *A Study in Scarlet*, he famously tells Watson, "'It is quite *a three pipe problem,* and I beg that you won't speak to me for fifty minutes.'" In *The Sign of Four*, Holmes does not have the luxury of time to consider the mystery in this way since as soon as Mary Morstan leaves his room he goes out to collect more data on her father's disappearance from the back-files of the *Times*. When he returns a few hours later, he is able to tell Watson:

> "There is no great mystery in this matter," he said, taking the cup of tea which I had poured out for him. "The facts appear to admit of only one explanation."
> "What! you have solved it already?"

"Well, that would be too much to say. I have discovered a
suggestive fact, that is all."

From the facts of Major Sholto's death on 28th of April, 1882, and Mary
Morstan having received the first pearl less than a week later, Holmes concludes
that Sholto's heir (whoever he may be) knows that Captain Morstan was
deprived of something very valuable by the Major and wishes to make restitution
to the man's only living heir. Challenged to provide "'an alternative theory that
will meet the facts,'" Watson is forced to admit that he cannot.

Holmes' complacency, however, suffers a succession of blows. Firstly, in
the cab to the Lyceum, Miss Morstan shows him the note signed by the Four.
Having studied it closely, Holmes is forced to "'confess that I do not see how
this bears upon the matter.'" In the remaining time that it takes the cab to get to
the Lyceum, Watson observes Holmes in deep thought, presumably trying to
reconcile this new data with the "explanation" he has already formulated, "He
leaned back in the cab, and I could see by his drawn brow and his vacant eye that
he was thinking intently."

The second blow to Holmes' complacency comes when the mystery of
Captain Morstan's disappearance, and of the pearls sent to his daughter, is
overtaken by the crime of murder. Unlike Inspector Jones, who will quickly
come up with a theory of the crime and do everything possible to make the
evidence conform to it, Holmes is always ready to re-evaluate his hypotheses: if
his narrative no longer covers the facts, he adapts his narrative. In this way, he is
able to integrate the death of Captain Morstan, the sending of the pearls, and the
murder of Bartholomew Sholto into a narrative which covers *all* of the fact.
Thus, after finding the dead body of Bartholomew Sholto, and specifically after
finding the poisoned dart which killed him, Holmes has his revised theory of the
crime complete:

"This is all an insoluble mystery to me," said I. "It grows
darker instead of clearer."

"On the contrary," he answered, "it clears every instant. I only
require a few missing links to have an entirely connected case."

One notes again Holmes' insufferable arrogance, but it is clear that, at this point,
he knows how: Major Sholto got his wealth; Bartholomew Sholto was murdered;
Jonathan Small entered Sholto's bedroom; the nature of his accomplice; and
Small and this accomplice got away with the treasure. The main missing links
are the details of Major Sholto's treachery over the treasure and the treasure's
origin - details which can only be given by Jonathan Small who was an
eyewitness to those events. There remains, however, the small matter of finding
the culprits and recovering the treasure, to some share of which Miss Morstan
appears to be entitled.

From this point on, scientific detection has to take a back seat to what the official police would call 'leg-work.' The use of the bloodhound is standard procedure; Holmes' questioning of Mrs. Smith is devious and effective; his employment of the Baker Street Irregulars is entirely sensible. All of this makes for an exciting yarn, but it hardly allows Holmes to display those 'scientific' powers of observation, knowledge and inference which set him apart as a detective. It is understandable that Holmes expresses his frustration to Watson, "'this infernal problem is consuming me. It is too much to be baulked by so petty an obstacle, when all else has been overcome. I know the men, the launch, everything, and yet I can get no news.'"

In fact, there is only one remaining mystery to solve: How can a steam launch completely disappear from view along a stretch of twenty miles (or so) of the most public waterway in the world? Holmes spends the entire night turning the riddle over in his mind. In the morning, he tells Watson, "'I have been turning it over in my mind, and I can see only one way out of it.'" Holmes' answer to that puzzle is an illustration of the maxim that he states to Watson early in the story when explaining how he deduces that Watson has been to the post office to send a telegram, "'Eliminate all other factors, and the one which remains must be the truth,'" and again later when he explains how he deduces the method by which the murderer entered Bartholomew Sholto's room, "'How often have I said to you that when you have eliminated the impossible whatever remains, *however improbable*, must be the truth.'" In the case of the vanishing boat, Holmes infers that, since the *Aurora* is not *on* the river (i.e. tied up at a wharf somewhere), it must either be *under* the water (i.e. scuttled), a possibility he considers very remote, or *in some way obscured from view* (i.e. in the shed or dry dock of a ship repairer hidden but available for use at short notice).

This conclusion can only be tested by more leg-work which Holmes undertakes to do himself in disguise, another strategy not open to the official police whose very status might cause potential informers to clam up. Since he is now looking in the right places, he is able to locate the *Aurora* in a matter of hours. When he explains his reasoning to Watson, Holmes points out that his success has been brought by following another principle that he explained early in the story concerning minutiae, "'It is just these very simple things which are extremely liable to be overlooked.'" As happens so often when Holmes explains how he has reached his conclusions, the answer appears (in retrospect) to be entirely obvious.

Holmes' confidence that Small and his accomplice will make their bid to escape the country at a particular time is necessarily less firmly based for there is no actual data. Although Holmes does not explicitly identify his deductive method, it is clearly an example of that which he explains to Watson in the short story "The Musgrave Ritual": "You know my method in such cases, Watson, I put myself in the man's place, and having gauged his intelligence, I try to imagine how I should myself have proceeded under the same circumstances."

This method depends on a pseudo-scientific determinism which, in Holmesian detection, is assumed to control and limit human behavior. Unlike the Musgrave case where his opponent, the butler Brunton, has a first-rate intelligence which frees Holmes from the need to "make any allowance for persona equation," Although Jonathan Small constantly surprises Holmes by showing an intelligence and ingenuity beyond what is natural to his class, the very success of Holmes' prediction about his attempt to escape vindicates Holmes' methods.

The Character of Sherlock Holmes

> How weary, stale, flat, and unprofitable
> Seem to me all the uses of this world!
> Fie on't, ah fie! 'tis an unweeded garden
> That grows to seed, things rank and gross in nature
> Possess it merely. (Shakespeare *Hamlet* 1.2.133-7)

Drug Addiction

> As a doctor, Conan Doyle was aware of the specific symptoms of cocaine usage and he gave them to Sherlock Holmes, who typically exhibited periods of prolonged sleep, general tiredness, occasional lassitude and mental depression. (Booth 148).

There is something of Hamlet's world-weariness in Sherlock Holmes: the commonplace world is too narrow for his mind which craves intellectual stimulation. When, as at the opening of the novel, crime offers no challenging problem, Holmes resorts to chemical stimulants.

O'Dell points out that the 1880s marked a period when, "The proliferation of cocaine and morphine use amongst the upper and middle classes as a result of medical experimentation and the appearance of the hypodermic syringe brought with it an unprecedented era in public knowledge of the risks associated with narcotic drugs." In contrast, Keep and Randall point out that, "By the mid-1880s, British medical journals were overflowing in their praise of cocaine's medicinal properties and Conan Doyle, himself a practicing physician at the time, is also known to have experimented with the drug." They go on to point out that, being published in 1890, *The Sign of Four* appeared just at the point where the medical establishment was beginning to perform "a remarkable volte-face concerning the therapeutic value of the drug. As its addictive properties became better known, cocaine was increasingly associated with the degenerative effects of opium use. The alkaloid effectively went from being a miracle of modern medicine to a vestigial horror of Europe's colonial enterprise." Dr. Watson is thus ahead of his time in warning of the dangers of cocaine use.

The precisely observed description, in the first paragraph of the novel, of Holmes preparing to inject himself is shocking even if we remember that drug-taking (or rather the taking of certain kinds of drugs) did not then have the negative connotations which it does today. Notice the contrast between the reassuring detail of the "neat morocco case" and the "delicate needle," and the graphic description of Holmes' forearm "dotted and scared with innumerable puncture-marks." Dr. Watson's concern with the long-term physical effects of cocaine appears to be fully justified by the evidence that he observes, and by the medical knowledge he has of resulting "'tissue-change'" leading to "'permanent weakness.'" To this is added his observation of the "black reaction" of depression and lethargy which is typically displaced by the euphoria induced by the drug. Against this, Holmes has only his psychological need of the "'transcendentally stimulating and clarifying'" effect of the drug on his mind, for which he is prepared to ignore the physical effects of long-term use. There is no doubt that Watson wins this argument.

Why should Doyle have chosen to show Holmes in this novel (as in *A Study in Scarlet*) to be psychologically dependent upon, though not physically addicted to, certain drugs? To understand this, we must put aside our contemporary conception of banned substances. Neither morphine nor cocaine were illegal at the time. Then, as now, an individual's drug of choice depended very much upon the related factors of income and social class. Booth points out that Doyle uses drug-taking as a way of elevating Holmes beyond the mainstream, the people who live lives of dull routine:

> The real reason why Conan Doyle made Sherlock Holmes an addict was not to give him a flawed character (addiction was not censured in Victorian times, as it was subsequently to become) or a particular foible. It was because he wanted his readers to view Holmes as an aesthete. Drug addiction had a romantic, artistic ring to it. Poets and writers, artists and musicians were, as the parlance had it, *habitués* , their habits a sign of their uniqueness and intellectual or even spiritual superiority. Drug addiction was an acceptable vice and few readers would have condemned Sherlock Holmes for his addiction ... Cocaine, the drug of preference of the upper classes or well-to-do, of which Conan Doyle accurately wrote, squarely outlining its stimulation of the mind, was exotic. (Booth 149)

Thus, Holmes' drug habit is intended as an indication of superior sensibility. Holmes' drug use marks him as an aesthete - one who is particularly sensitive to and appreciative of the beautiful in art (Holmes plays the violin and frequently attends classical concerts). He is a connoisseur of crime.

In further mitigation may be added the argument of F. A. Allen that a 7% solution was "moderate and even therapeutic" (Klinger ed. 215). By the time that Doyle began writing short stories featuring Holmes, medical opinion was entirely hostile to the therapeutic use of cocaine and morphine, and so he ensured that Watson's attempts to wean his friend off stimulants were largely successful, though there was the constant danger of relapse. In fact, there are only five references in the entire canon to Holmes' drug use.

The Rational, Emotionless Man?

> To Sherlock Holmes she is always *the* woman. I have seldom heard him mention her under any other name. In his eyes she eclipses and predominates the whole of her sex. It was not that he felt any emotion akin to love for Irene Adler. All emotions, and that one particularly, were abhorrent to his cold, precise but admirably balanced mind. ("A Scandal In Bohemia" original emphasis)

With the single exception of Irene Adler, the one woman to defeat him intellectually, Holmes' misogyny (dislike of women) is a fixed feature of his character. It is evident in *The Sign of Four* both in his statement to Watson following the first interview with Miss Morstan that he did not notice her beauty and in his reaction to Watson's announcement of his engagement. In the case of the former, Holmes argues that appearances are no guide to character and should therefore be excluded from consideration and of the latter that love, being "an emotional thing … is opposed to that true cold reason which I place above all things." Caprettini explains how Holmes' attitude to women is simply part of his "theoretical need" for clarity:

> [If] the detective wants his mind to be the mirror of that sequence of causes and effects which ended in a crime, he must get rid of every subjective element of nuisance. The logical purity of his reason should not be disturbed by feeling and pathos. The woman, who has the power of starting illogical (that is, passionate) mechanisms in man's mind, must be strictly excluded from the sphere of analytical and abductive reasoning (Hodgson ed. 331)

Holmes insists that, "'Detection is, or ought to be, an exact science, and should be treated in the same cold and unemotional manner.'" The most important phrase in that statement is the qualifier "'or ought to be,'" for the truth is that Holmes is not so unemotional as he would like to believe himself to be, nor as he endeavors to appear. He clearly desires to reduce life to a process of "'analytical reasoning from effects to causes,'" but he knows that life cannot be so simplified.

The most obvious example of his dismissive manner is seen in his being unable (i.e., unwilling) to congratulate Watson on either his book *A Study in Scarlet* or on his plans to marry. However, that this does not define the whole man is the obvious concern and affection which he has for Watson. Notice, for example, his profuse apology when he realizes that his concentration on the problem of deducing from a watch the circumstances and personality of its owner leads him to say something thoughtless and hurtful about Watson's brother. In addition, many of the things that Holmes says are for effect. It is easy to miss the humor of those statements which are meant to shock the gullible Watson.

The Character of Dr. Watson

> Any studies in Sherlock Holmes must be, first and foremost, studies in Dr. Watson. (Knox, Bloom ed. 75)

As narrator, Watson is, of course, writing after the conclusion of each case when he already knows the solution to the mystery, but in order to function as an effective narrative device whereby Doyle can keep the reader in suspense as to the solution, he must limit himself to recording what he experienced *as he experienced it*. In this way, he provides most (though not always quite all) of the clues which Holmes will use to solve the mystery without differentiating between those details which are and those which are not significant. Watson sees everything but understands nothing: he is frequently puzzled, sometimes reaches too quickly for the obvious, and often, when attempting to imitate the deductive thinking of his brilliant friend, arrives at an absolutely wrong conclusion even though he is reasoning from the same data as Holmes.

The reader identifies with Watson in a way that would not be possible with Holmes. As Cox writes:

> Watson is human when Holmes is cold and indifferent, and readers no doubt sense in this rather practical physician the touch of humanity that makes him trustworthy. The reader can believe in these adventures because he knows that Watson reports them without exaggeration. In short, Watson reacts the way a reader might in his shoes; one therefore identifies with his point of view. (Cox 183)

That Watson is a romantic is evidenced by the parts of *A Study in Scarlet* to which Holmes objects - undoubtedly the long and sensational flashback in Part Two: "The Country of the Saints" which is actually the sort of historical adventure that Doyle preferred to write.

Opposites Attract

In many ways, Dr. Watson is Holmes' opposite: Holmes is a thinker, Watson a man of action; Holmes is a rationalist, Watson a romantic; Holmes lives only for the opportunity to solve the most complex of crimes, Watson has a full, well-rounded life. Where Holmes hides his feeling for Watson, Watson speaks directly of his sense of concern for Holmes as a "'comrade'" and as a "'a medical man'" who bears some responsibility for Holmes' health. Watson clearly holds his friend in awe and respect, aware of his superior intellectual powers and unwilling ever to do anything that would offend him. At the same time, Watson is aware of what he ironically calls Holmes' "small vanity," and is irritated by the "somewhat dogmatic tone" with which Holmes frequently addresses him.

British Colonialism

> For his period, Doyle caught in the Holmes stories an ensemble of attitudes, of fears and hopes. For anyone interested in seeing how dominant social groups use their literature to state and control fears, the Holmes stories are a fascinating source. They provide a means of recreating the structure of feeling in a complex period ... (Stephen King in Hodgson ed. 379)

In three of the four novels (the exception is *The Hound of the Baskervilles*) violence and murder are brought to England from outside. In *A Study in Scarlet*, a murder in an abandoned house off the Brixton Road has its origins in the Mormon Church in Utah; in *The Valley of Fear*, a murder at Birlstone originates in an under-cover operation against a corrupt union in the Vermissa coal mine area of the western U.S.A.. In the case of The *Sign of Four*, however, murder has its origins in India where simple desire for wealth leads to dishonor, death and ultimately murder which threatens established middle-class order:

> Holmes's work first traces, then contains and controls, the disruptive colonial contaminations of metropolitan space; this mastering of disorder is signified, most notably, by the detective's production of narrative closure. (Keep and Randall)

As has been made clear in the Commentary, the novel embodies an ambiguous attitude to the British Empire. On the one hand, there is pride in the power of Britain to subjugate native peoples around the globe forming an Empire on which the sun never set, but on the other hand there is a fear, amounting to paranoia, of foreign influence undermining the British character. As in Conrad's *Heart of Darkness*, London represents the center of Empire, but whilst in Conrad Europeans go outward from the capital to explore and civilize the dark places of the world, in *The Sign of Four* the emphasis is on those who return having been corrupted by their experience.

Taylor-Ide explains:

> Victorian social theorists from Marx to Mill equated foreign lands with prior stages of evolution. Thus, it is not surprising that in many of Holmes's cases ,and every one that deals with the apparently super natural, this struggle between the human and animal is directly connected to foreign lands. Often, as in *The Sign of Four*, these cases bring to light dark secrets lying behind apparently legitimate fortunes that were brought home from abroad, where the crime under investigation is in fact retribution for wrongs

The Sign of Four by Sir Arthur Conan Doyle

committed overseas.

Against the passions exposed by the East, stands Holmes as the representative of reason, logic and civilization who will beat back the tide of Tonga's animalism and the consequences of Sholto's dishonorable and criminal actions.

Appendix One: Brief Summaries of the Other Sherlock Holmes Novels

Note: The following summaries *do not* give the solutions to the mysteries that Holmes' investigates in each novel.

A Study in Scarlet

Inspector Gregson of Scotland Yard takes Holmes and Watson to the scene of a murder: a man has been poisoned but not robbed, and the word "RACHE" (German for revenge) has been written in blood on the wall. The police make an arrest, but when a second murder occurs it is clear that they have the wrong man. Holmes' investigation uncovers a feud linked to the Mormon community in Salt Lake City, U.S.A..

The Hound of the Baskervilles

The suspicious death of Sir Charles Baskerville recalls for his friend Dr. Mortimer the Baskerville curse: as revenge for the vile cruelties of Hugo Baskerville each male heir will be haunted by an avenging hound. Dr. Mortimer consults Holmes about how to protect the new heir, Sir Henry, when he arrives from Canada. Holmes sends Watson to stay with Sir Henry at Baskerville Hall, but his own investigations reveal a plot even more terrible that the huge hound which stalks Dartmoor.

The Valley of Fear

Inspector MacDonald of Scotland Yard calls upon Holmes to ask for his help in investigating the murder of Mr. Douglas of Birlstone Manor House. Working on an inside tip, Holmes tells the Inspector that he suspects that Professor Moriarty is somehow connected with the murder. Holmes' investigation reveals that Douglas' real name is Birdy Edwards and that he was a detective with the Pinkerton Detective Agency. The mystery of Edwards' death is intimately connected with his undercover work in the Vermissa Valley, U.S.A..

Appendix Two: Character Traits (Student Activities)

On the following pages, identify the character traits for each person (some of which are done for you), explain each trait and note an example in the text.

Character of Sherlock Holmes

Arrogant

Obsessive

Easily bored

Sherlock Holmes as Detective

Observant

Logical

Unemotional

The Sign of Four by Sir Arthur Conan Doyle

Character of Dr. Watson

Caring

Modest

Romantic

_____

_____

_____

Appendix Three: The Scientific Detective (Student Activities)

The following pages present in a graphic format the thinking of Sherlock Holmes on the various problems presented to him in the course of the novel.

1. Two Examples of the Methods of Sherlock Holmes in Chapter One

How Holmes deduces that Watson has been to the Post-Office to send a telegram.

Observation	+	Knowledge	=	Deduction
Watson's shoe has "a little _____ _____."		a) The pavement is being repaved on _____ _____.		Watson went to the Post-Office.
		b) One has to walk on the earth to get into the Post-Office		
		c) The earth is _____ _____		
Watson has not written a letter that morning. Watson has a stock of _____ _____		None.		Watson can only have gone to the Post-Office to _____ _____ _____

The Sign of Four by Sir Arthur Conan Doyle

Chapter One (continued):

What Holmes deduces from an examination of Watson's pocket watch.

Observation:
The watch is fifty years old.
Deduction:
It originally belonged to

_____

and was inherited by

_____

Observation:
"H.W." is engraved on the back of the watch.
Deduction:

"W" stands for

_____

Observation:
Dents in two places on the watch case.
Deduction:

Its owner

_____

_____

_____

Observation:
Thousands of tiny scratches around the key-hole.
Deduction:

_____

_____

_____

Observation:
The watch is expensive (fifty guineas) and it has tiny numbers engraved on the inside of the case.
Knowledge:
Pawnbrokers do this to identify items

Deduction:

_____

_____

2. The History of the Crime

Chapter Two:

Clues	Possible Deductions
Major Sholto and Captain Morstan were prison officers of the Andaman Islands. Major Sholto retired to Norwood.	The key to the mystery is something that happened on the Andaman Islands. _____ _____.
Captain Morstan returned to England on one year's leave. He appears to have been in a very positive frame of mind.	His reason for his visit home was to claim his share of the treasure which he was anxious to share with his daughter.
Dec 3rd, 1878 - Having left the Langham Hotel the previous evening, Morstan fails to return and was never seen again.	_____ _____
Major Sholto claimed not to know that Captain Morstan had returned to England and not to have seen him.	Since Major Sholto was the only person Captain Morstan knew in London, this seems unlikely, so Sholto is lying.
May 4th, 1882 - An advertisement is placed in the _Times_ requesting the address of Miss Morstan. 1882 to 1886 - Miss Morstan receives a valuable pearl sent anonymously each year.	Someone has just discovered that Miss Morstan has been cheated out of a great deal of money. _____ _____

July 7th, 1888 - Miss Morstan receives an anonymous letter calling her a "wronged woman" and appointing a time and place for a meeting.

Something has happened which makes Miss Morstan's anonymous benefactor

_____

_____

_____.

The writing of the addresses on the pearl box is

_____

_____

_____.

Chapter Three:

Clues	Possible Deductions
April 25th, 1882 - Major John Sholto died. May 4th, 1882 - An advertisement in the Times was closely followed by delivery of the first of the six pearls.	The person who communicates with Miss Morstan knows _____ _____.
Major Sholto was "'a very particular friend'" of Captain Morstan.	_____ _____.
A paper was found in Captain Morstan's desk containing the plan of a large building, a small red cross, and the names of "the four" (one English name and three Indian names)..	The diagram certainly looks like a treasure map (x marks the spot). The Four must therefore be the men who had hidden the treasure.

The Sign of Four by Sir Arthur Conan Doyle

Chapter Four:

Clues	Deductions
Major Sholto returned from India with "a considerable sum of money, and a large collection of valuable curiosities." He bought a house and lived in great luxury.	The only way an army officer could return from India with great wealth would be
Major Sholto took extraordinary measures to ensure his own safety and security.	He lived in constant fear of whoever he had stolen the treasure from - presumably
Major Sholto had a mortal fear of men with a wooden leg. He attacks a perfectly innocent man simply because he has this handicap.	One of The Four was a man with a wooden leg. This person must be
1882 Major Sholto received "a letter from India which was a great shock to him."	Presumably the letter informed Sholto that the one-legged man had been released, or had escaped from, the prison on the Andaman Islands.

April 5th, 1882 Major Sholto's death-bed confession:	His story confirms most previous deductions.

- he and Captain Morstan came into possession of a considerable treasure;

- Captain Morstan came to England to claim his share but they quarreled.

- Captain Morstan had a heart attack during the argument with Major Sholto on how to divide the treasure;

- Major Sholto hides the body that night.

At the moment he was about to reveal to his two sons where the treasure was hidden, Sholto saw a face at the window which literally scared him to death. This man had a wooden leg.	Major Sholto recognized the man. The man was _____
On the next morning an intruder searched the Major's room. He left a note saying "The sign of the four" on the Major's dead body.	He was looking for _____ He found _____

3. Examining the Scene of the Crime

Chapter Five: *Bartholomew Sholto's Room*

Observation	Knowledge	Deduction
There is a hole broken into the ceiling and a set of steps giving access to the garret.		_____ _____ .
_____ is found on the table.		The accomplice is a primitive native from the Far East. The Andaman Islands would be the logical conclusion.
A note is found on the table with "The Sign of Four" "scrawled upon it"		The note was hurriedly written by _____

Chapter Six:

Observation	Knowledge	Deduction
The door is locked and bolted from the inside.	Parallel cases from India and Senegambia	The other intruder _____ _____
The window has been locked from the inside.		Ditto...
It would be impossible to climb the sixty feet up to the window unaided.		Ditto...

A Study Guide

Observation	Knowledge	Deduction
Evidence on the window sill shows that a man has entered/ left by the window.		Ditto...
There is a footmark and a "circular muddy mark."		The intruder was a _____
The rope shows evidence of skin rubbed from a man's hands		Caused when the intruder (who does not have the hard hands of a sailor) descended the rope
Prints of a small, naked foot.	Holmes recalls a similar case that explains the small footprints.	Since there is only the print of one foot, the person must have stepped in something.
The "thorn" is not English.		It is from the Far East.
The "thorn" which killed Bartholomew has a "gummy" substance on its point.		It is _____ _____
The puncture wound in the victim lines up with the hole in the ceiling.		The murderer was in the garret and shot his dart through the hole in the ceiling.

The Sign of Four by Sir Arthur Conan Doyle

Chapter Seven:

The Garret and the Roof

Observation	Knowledge	Deduction
The footprints in the garret show that "each toe is distinctly divided."		_____ _____
A pouch of woven grasses is found that contains "half a dozen spines of dark wood."		_____ _____

Finding the Fugitives and the Treasure

Once Holmes learns, through his skillful questioning of Mrs. Mordecai Smith, that Jonathan Small and his accomplice made their escape on the *Aurora*, and that the steam boat has not returned to the boatyard, the investigation appears to have reached a dead end. Finding the fugitives is no longer merely an intellectual puzzle, the extensive waterfront on both banks of the river has to be searched, and for this Holmes utilizes the Baker Street Irregulars. This is not to say, however, that logic does not guide the actions that Holmes himself, for when (in an appropriate disguise) he sets out to find the *Aurora* he locates it relatively quickly because reasoning has indicated *where* he should look.

Chapter Eight

Watson's suggestions	*Holmes' rejections*
Hire a launch and search down river for the Aurora.	
_____.	Entirely illogically, Holmes has "'a fancy for working it out for myself.'" This is pure vanity.
_____.	This would alert the culprits who would immediately leave the country. They will stay hidden in London while ever they feel safe.
	(Note that Holmes will later revise his view of using an advertisement - yet another example of his flexible approach to investigations.)

The Sign of Four by Sir Arthur Conan Doyle

Possible explanations for the Disappearance of the Aurora

Chapter Nine

Possibilities	Holmes' assessment
It is moored at a wharf below London Bridge. It could be on either the North or South Bank.	_____ _____.
It is moored above London Bridge. It has been scuttled.	Holmes extends the search up-river. _____ _____ _____.
It is in a boatyard undergoing minor (and unnecessary) repairs.	This would explain why the boat is not in plain sight

How to Catch Jonathan Small

Chapters Nine and Ten

Possibilities	Holmes' assessment
Jonathan Small and his accomplice have already left the country.	Small would need some time to _____..
They _____ _____..	The appearance of this accomplice is too distinctive to avoid notice during their escape in the morning. They must get away.
They will make a break for it by taking the Aurora down river to get on a ship and leave the country.	Holmes describes this as "the balance of probability." It is, of course, confirmed when at Jacobsen's Yard he hears Mordecai Smith order the boat to be ready for 8 p.m. that day.

Guide to Further Reading

Biography

Martin Booth's *The Doctor and the Detective: A Biography of Sir Arthur Conan Doyle* is a fascinating look into the life of the man who created Sherlock Holmes (and who firmly believed in the existence of fairies).

Detective Fiction in General

P. D. James' *Talking About Detective Fiction* is a readable introduction to the whole genre. The early chapters deal with the development of the detective mystery genre, and Holmes has a chapter almost to himself.

The Sherlock Holmes Stories

Doyle and Crowder's *Sherlock Holmes for Dummies* provides a general introduction to Holmes and his creator, but has nothing detailed on *The Sign of Four*.

The Lyle Thorne Mysteries:

If you enjoy the Sherlock Holmes stories, allow me to recommend a series of books written by myself. Each book features five cases featuring The Reverend Lyle Thorne, Vicar of Sanditon. The stories take place between 1876 and 1940:

> *Investigations of The Reverend Lyle Thorne*
> *Further Investigations of The Reverend Lyle Thorne*
> *Early Investigations of Lyle Thorne*
> *Sanditon Investigations of The Reverend Lyle Thorne*
> *Final Investigations of The Reverend Lyle Thorne (to be published   2015)*

Biography

Booth, Martin, *The Doctor and the Detective: A Biography of Sir Arthur Conan Doyle*. 1st edition. New York: Thomas Dunn Books, 2000. Print.

Critical Works on Detective Fiction

Bloom, Harold ed. Classic Mystery Writers. 1st edition. New York: Chelsea House,1995. Print.
James, P. D., *Talking About Detective Fiction*. 1st edition. New York: Alfred A. Knopf 2009. Print.
Knight, *Stephen. Crime Fiction 1800-2000*. 1st edition. Basingstoke: Palgrave Macmillan, 2004. Print.

The Sign of Four by Sir Arthur Conan Doyle

Critical Works on Sherlock Holmes

Cox, Richard. *Arthur Conan Doyle. New York*: 1st edition. Frederick Ungar, 1985. Print.
Doyle, Steven and David A. Crowder. *Sherlock Holmes for Dummies.* 1st edition. New Jersey Wiley Publishing, 2010. Print.
Hodgson, John. *Arthur Conan Doyle Sherlock Holmes: The Major Stories with Contemporary Critical Essays.* 1st edition. Boston: Bedford Books, 1994. Print.
Jann, Rosemary. *The Adventures of Sherlock Holmes: Detecting Social Order.* 1st edition. New York: Twayne, 1995. Print.
Pearsall, Roland. *Conan Doyle: A Biographical Solution.* 1977. 1st edition. London: Weidenfield and Nicholson, 1977. Print.

Critical Essays on Sherlock Holmes

Bertman, Stephen. "Poe's 'The Murders in the Rue Morgue' and Doyle's *The Sign of Four*." *Edgar Allan Poe Review* 15.2 (2014): 205-210. Print. Clausson, Nils. "The case of the anomalous narrative: gothic 'surmise' and trigonometric 'proof' in Arthur Conan Doyle's 'The Musgrave Ritual.'" Victorian Newsletter 107 (2005): 5-10. Print.
Farrell, Kirby. "Heroism, culture, and dread in *The Sign of Four*." *Studies in the Novel* 16 (1984): 32-51. Print.
Keep, Christopher and Don Randall. "Action, empire, and narrative in Arthur Conan Doyle's *The Sign of Four*." *Novel: A Forum on Fiction Spring* 32.2 (1999): 207-221. Print.
Neilson, Keith. "*The Sign of Four*." *Masterplots*. Salem Press (2010): 1-4. Print.
O'Dell, Benjamin. "Performing the Imperial Abject: The Ethics of Cocaine in Arthur Conan Doyle's *The Sign of Four*." *Journal of Popular Culture* 45.5 (2012): 979-999. Print.
Taylor-Ide, Jesse. "Ritual and the Liminality of Sherlock Holmes in *The Sign of Four* and 'The Hound of the Baskervilles.'" *English Literature in Transition: 1880-1920* 48.1 (2005) 55-70. Print.

Internet

Fraser, Jennifer. "Imperial Contradictions in Arthur Conan Doyle's 'The Sign of Four.'" *Studies by Undergraduate Researchers at Guelph*. University of Guelph, 1 Jan. 2012. Web. 28 Nov. 2014.

To the Reader

Ray strives to make his products the best that they can be. If you have any comments or question about this book *please* contact the author through his email: **moore.ray1@yahoo.com**

Visit his website at **http://www.raymooreauthor.com**

Also by Ray Moore:

All books are available from amazon.com and from barnesandnoble.com as paperbacks and at most online eBook retailers.

Fiction:

The Lyle Thorne Mysteries: each book features five tales from the Golden Age of Detection:

> *Investigations of The Reverend Lyle Thorne*
> *Further Investigations of The Reverend Lyle Thorne*
> *Early Investigations of Lyle Thorne*
> *Sanditon Investigations of The Reverend Lyle Thorne*

Non-fiction:- listed alphabetically by author

The ***Critical Introduction series*** is written for high school teachers and students and for college undergraduates. Each volume gives an in-depth analysis of a key text:

> *"Pride and Prejudice" by Jane Austen: A Critical Introduction*
> *"The Stranger" by Albert Camus: A Critical Introduction (Revised Edition)*
> *"The General Prologue" by Geoffrey Chaucer: A Critical Introduction*
> *"The Great Gatsby" by F. Scott Fitzgerald: A Critical Introduction*

The Text and Critical Introduction series differs from the Critical introduction series as these books contain the original medieval text together with an interlinear translation to aid the understanding of the text. The commentary allows the reader to develop a deeper understanding of the text and themes within the text.

> *"The General Prologue" by Geoffrey Chaucer: Text and Critical Introduction*
> *"The Wife of Bath's Prologue and Tale" by Geoffrey Chaucer: Text and Critical Introduction*
> *"Sir Gawain and the Green Knight": Text and Critical Introduction*
> *"Heart of Darkness" by Joseph Conrad: Text and Critical Introduction*
> *"The Sign of Four" by Sir Arthur Conan Doyle: Text and Critical Introduction*

The Sign of Four by Sir Arthur Conan Doyle

Study guides available in print

"Wuthering Heights" by Emily Brontë: A Study Guide
"Great Expectations" by Charles Dickens: A Study Guide
"A Room with a View" by E. M. Forster: A Study Guide
"An Inspector Calls" by J.B. Priestley: A Study Guide
"Macbeth" by William Shakespeare: A Study Guide
"Othello" by William Shakespeare: A Study Guide
"The Myth of Sisyphus" and "The Stranger" by Albert Camus: Two Study Guides

Study Guides available as e-books:

"Jane Eyre" by Charlotte Brontë: A Study Guide
"Wuthering Heights" by Emily Brontë: A Study Guide
"The Myth of Sisyphus" and "The Stranger" by Albert Camus: Two Study Guides
"Heart of Darkness" by Joseph Conrad: A Study Guide
"Great Expectations" by Charles Dickens: A Study Guide
"The Mill on the Floss" by George Eliot: A Study Guide
"Lord of the Flies" by William Golding: A Study Guide
"Catch-22" by Joseph Heller: A Study Guide
"Life of Pi" by Yann Martel: A Study Guide
"Nineteen Eighty-Four" by George Orwell: A Study Guide
"Selected Poems" by Sylvia Plath: A Study Guide
"Henry IV Part 2" by William Shakespeare: A Study Guide
"Julius Caesar" by William Shakespeare: A Study Guide
"Macbeth" by William Shakespeare: A Study Guide
"Antigone" by Sophocles: A Study Guide
"Of Mice and Men" by John Steinbeck: A Study Guide
"The Pearl" by John Steinbeck: A Study Guide
"Slaughterhouse-Five" by Kurt Vonnegut: A Study Guide
"The Bridge of San Luis Rey" by Thornton Wilder: A Study Guide

Teacher resources:

Ray also publishes ***many more*** study guides and other resources for classroom use on the 'Teacher Pay Teachers' website:

http://www.teacherspayteachers.com/Store/Raymond-Moore

Printed in Great Britain
by Amazon